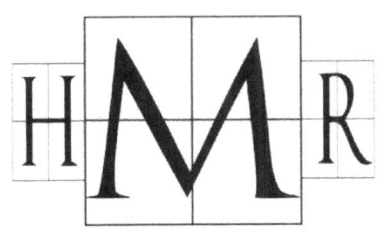

Hunger Moon

Hot Moon Rising Book 7

By
Merryn Dexter

Copyright © 2016 by Merryn Dexter
ISBN: 978-1-68361-053-3
Cover art by Mina Carter

Published by Decadent Publishing Company, LLC
Look for us online at:
www.decadentpublishing.com

~A Note from the Author~

Dear Reader

I am so pleased to be working again with the amazing Decadent Publishing team – dreams really do come true! My imagination is fired up so I hope to be able to bring you many more stories in partnership with them. I had so much fun playing in the fabulous world of the Moonlight pack while writing Silver Moon that I couldn't wait to return.

Troy and Bel certainly put me through the emotional wringer, but the best kind of love stories are the ones you have to fight hard for.

I would be thrilled to hear from you about this book, Hot Moon Rising, Wiccan Haus, the Black Hills Wolves, soup recipes, holidays, or anything else that crosses your mind. I'm a military spouse currently resident in Belgium and working from home so always happy for a distraction!

You can email me at merryn.dexter@yahoo.com or find me on Facebook or Twitter @MerrynDexter. I also have a website www.merryndexter.com and a blog www.merryndexter.blogspot.be.

Best Wishes
Merryn x

Dedication

For M. Who brings a little bit of magic into my life every day.

Moonlight Wolf Pack

Charlie Aquino (human) – Detective for the sheriff's gang task force for Palmetto County Sheriff's Department. His partner is Jesse Farrell.
- Mate: Liana Cosa

Liana Cosa Aquino – Refugee from a different pack. She works part-time as a waitress at Moonlight Diner.
- Mate: Charlie Aquino

Silver Ellis (human) – Was the witness of a violent crime and placed in Kirk's protection as a favor to Jesse Farrell and Charlie Aquino. Works as a school teacher.
- Mate: Kirk Matheson

Alexa Martin Farrell – Left her pack over a disagreement with her alpha. She moved to Florida and helped the pack find a small community of cottages in Moonlight, Florida. She works as an Internet researcher and gets jobs through her online website. She also does research for The Defenders.
- Mate: Jesse Farrell

Jesse Farrell (human) – Detective for the sheriff's gang task force for Palmetto County Sheriff's Department. His partner is Charlie Aquino.
- Mate: Alexa Martin (who saved him when on assignment he was attacked by a gang)

Riesa Marlowe (human) – A psychic who helped locate Hannah Raines.
- Mate: Derek Sawyer

Kirk Matheson – Works for The Defenders Agency. Has a cabin offset in the woods, about a mile from town.
- Mate: Silver Ellis

Hannah Raines Molina – She was kidnapped and saved by Jesse and Charlie with the help of Riesa Marlowe, a psychic. Works as Alexa Martin's research assistant.
- Mate: Rand Molina

Rand Molina - Derek's second-in-command in the Moonlight pack. Partners with Derek Sawyer at The Defenders, a private security agency.
- Mate: Hannah Raines

Derek Sawyer – Alpha of a small pack. Most of their original clan was destroyed when developers took the land they were living on and many of their pack were killed by hunters. They hid in an abandoned orange grove until Alexa offered them the bungalows in exchange for their help. He and the others have embraced Jesse and Alexa and Charlie and Liana and given the female shifters a new sense of belonging.
- Partners with Rand Molina at The Defenders Agency, a private security and bodyguard agency.
- Mate: Riesa Marlowe

Alan Shifflett - When shifted, Alan appears with snaggled teeth and missing patches of hair. He's prone to violent outbursts. His teeth tear his lips, leaving wounds when he shifts. His father owns Moonlight Diner, which he is currently managing. He is also a programmer.
- Mate: Shelley Fields

The Defenders Agency - A private security and bodyguard agency formed by Rand and Derek once they were established in the little enclave of cottages. It provides good income for the pack. A majority of the pack is involved in the cases they take.
Jesse and Charlie are their contacts with the sheriff's department and also refer many cases to them.

Chapter One

Troy Lansing paused outside the door of his adopted father's study and sucked in a deep breath. He held it for a count of ten, listening to Clark raving about whatever latest event had riled his legendary temper. He could walk away, pretend he hadn't received the demand for his presence. Could find a warm and willing female and lose himself in a sweaty tangle of limbs. Could get in his car and keep driving until he hit the state line and escaped the daily madness of his life among the Brighton pack.

A dull thud impacted the other side of the heavy wooden door, followed by a groan of pain. *Shit!* Once Clark got physical no one in the vicinity was likely to escape unscathed. Glass crashed and a high-pitched cry sent Troy slamming through the door. He scanned the room, taking in the scene of devastation. His father's desk had been upended. Papers, folders, and the pretentious gold fountain pen set Clark used lay strewn across the thick Persian rug. A black stain decorated one wall, the viscous ink pooling against the baseboard like spilled blood. Diamond shards of glass winked in the dark ink, the remnants of the crystal inkwell Quinn had presented to Clark for his birthday.

Quinn.

Troy schooled his face to neutral as he studied the beginnings of a livid bruise on his sister's left cheek. Green eyes, a mirror to his own, reflected his blank stare. Never one to be cowed by the worst of Clark's outbursts, she stood at their father's left hand. He let his eyes slide past her, noting the pursed lips of the man standing closer to Quinn than her own shadow. Nikolas, another of Clark's adopted strays, served as the alpha's hammer, a title his father gave him where others might choose protector or enforcer. Family he might be, but Nik was no brother to Troy. His father's other "son," Dutton, slumped unconscious at Troy's feet having obviously lost his fight with the door.

Clark Lansing stood in the center of the chaos, graying hair hanging across his forehead, lungs working like a set of bellows as he snorted and raged like a Pamplonan bull. The madness clouding his black eyes cleared when he fixed on Troy. "Where the fuck have you been?" he snarled.

"I'm here now." He edged his voice with defiance. Let the alpha focus on him. Let Troy be the needle to lance the putrid boil of their father's rage. The scent of his sister's blood strained his control to the limits. He needed her out of the room before his wolf snapped the steel chains in which he'd bound his other half. Stepping over the fallen man, he closed the distance between himself and Clark, near enough to be perceived as a threat. He kept moving, forcing his father to shift position until he'd turned his back on Quinn. Troy tucked his hands in the front pockets of his slacks, an insolent gesture he paired with the easy smile that served as the cornerstone of his reputation for charm. *Now. Do it now, you nasty bastard.*

Keeping his eyes fixed on the alpha, he sent the force of his will toward Nikolas. Moving fast for a man of his immense size, the hammer clamped one hand over Quinn's mouth and the other around her waist, carrying her from the room as though she weighed nothing. Tension seeped from Troy. The inevitable beating to come would be acceptable now he knew she was out of the firing line. Had Dutton been conscious they could've worn down Clark's anger between them, but Troy was on his own.

The first blow rocked him on his heels. Hot iron burst in his mouth, and he turned his head to spit blood onto the ruined rug. His father snarled. Eyes glittering, he lowered into a fighting stance. Sometimes drawing blood would be enough to satisfy the alpha. Not today, though. Troy copied him. Removing his hands from his pockets, he slipped off his flat-soled shoes and flexed his toes against the thick carpet. The shards of glass would be a minor irritant compared to the payoff of better balance and speed.

"You think you can best me?" Clark sneered. Feinting to the left, he swung with his right, the blow glancing off Troy's jaw as he turned his face with the momentum of the strike.

"I know I can't, Alpha." He kicked out, catching the side of Clark's knee, sending him staggering. Even if he could beat the faster, stronger man, Troy didn't have what it took to lead a pack. He had dominance in spades but maintained enough self-awareness to acknowledge he lacked the special spark of a true alpha wolf. If he took Clark out, the pack would likely implode in a storm of blood and pain. The tentative bonds of peace between their disparate members relied on the alpha's tight fist to hold them. The best he could do for now was channel the worst of Clark's madness toward him. Troy cared about the pack. His beta-nature drove his need to protect and shield them. The cuts and bruises he gained today would heal soon enough. The scar tissue on his soul lay so thick another layer wouldn't make much difference.

A burning stripe of pain flashed across his chest. Blood welled between the tattered ruins of his shirt, thanks to the alpha's claws. Troy threw his head back, releasing a roar of pain. He hated to give even a hint of his suffering, but he knew it would help to satisfy the demon in Clark that loved to hurt. They traded heavy blows. The wolf in Troy would not allow him to take the punishment without responding, but, unlike his father, he had enough control to avoid striking his face. Hard knuckles impacted his kidneys, and bile surged in the back of his throat. Distracted, he misjudged his own strike, leaving himself open to a roundhouse kick. Blood poured from his split eyebrow, obscuring his vision. Clark yipped in excitement, and Troy dropped to one knee. The scents of copper and sweat swirled in the air, feeding the alpha's addiction. *Let it be enough.*

Lowering his head, he tried to calm his rapid pulse. His wolf snarled, desperate to fight back, furious he might yield when they had strength left. The alpha leaned close, the rough edge of his tongue lapping at the wound on Troy's forehead. Hot breath panted in his ear, and he schooled his gut not to rebel and unload its contents.

He could hear Quinn screaming from the other side of the door, the deep rumble of Nikolas's responses. The thick wood muffled the details of their conversation, but he knew she would be demanding entry. Nikolas protected Quinn, even from herself. It was his job. A task set him by the alpha at the first hints of her gaining maturity. He dogged her heels, cramped her style, and generally drove her crazy. Troy would have had no issue with it except for one thing—Nikolas served Clark with absolute loyalty and would kill Quinn if ordered to. A fact the alpha used to taunt and torture them all. *Divide and conquer*, the motto of the Brighton pack, was played out in gruesome technicolor within the alpha's immediate family.

A calloused hand cupped his cheek. Tears of impotent rage burned behind his eyes as warm fingers stroked his face, drawing him forward until Troy leaned against Clark's strong torso. Love, hatred, and resentment swirled through him, and he clenched his fists at his sides, fighting the urge to throw his arms around his father's waist and cling to him. This had been his life for too many years, and he needed to find a way to break free, before it destroyed them all.

***

Ignoring the prickle of broken glass in his heel, Troy took his seat at the dining table. Freshly showered and shaved, Clark sat at the head of the shiny walnut rectangle, a beatific smile on his face.

His approving gaze drifted around the table, pausing to rest on each of his four children. Troy didn't return his smile. There was nothing to smile about, and he didn't want to reopen the split in his lip. The cut over his eye had stopped bleeding, but the upper lid had swollen to the point he had no vision on his left side. He followed Clark's gaze, turning his head to regard Dutton who sat beside him. They had coaxed him into a shift after he regained consciousness, and Troy was relieved to note his pallor had lost the sickly green taint. A fractured skull could do that to a man. Without the healing powers of their wolf nature, not one of them would have survived their father's brutal idea of parenting.

Clark reached for his glass, raising the slender flute of champagne before him in a silent toast. Four matching glasses lifted in response. The sharp, clean zest of alcohol flooded Troy's mouth, washing away the sour bile. Quinn tipped her own glass steadily, draining the contents in a single draw. Nikolas touched his drink to his lips and returned it to the wrought silver coaster next to his bone-china plate. He stretched a thick arm across the table, the sleeve of his shirt inching back to reveal an intricate tattooed band at his wrist. Grasping the bottle, he refilled Quinn's glass, returning her nod of acknowledgment. The stilted display of manners between them stoically ignored the deep grooves she scratched in his cheek during her battle to get back into the study earlier.

A pair of submissive females entered the room, placed cold starters before each of them, and fled the room on silent feet. Clark ran his pack like some kind of ancient feudal lord, demanding absolute loyalty from his dominants and servitude from the submissives. Troy and the others waited for their father to lift his silverware before they turned their attention to the food before them. They ate in silence for a few moments. A part of his mind acknowledged the excellent quality of the meal, but the majority of his attention stayed focused on the alpha. He still didn't know what had triggered the fit of rage.

Placing his knife and fork together, Clark patted his lips with the crisp linen napkin from his lap then steepled his fingers over the empty plate. "Dutton. Share your news with Troy," he instructed. His calm, reasonable tone sent warning bells ringing in Troy's head.

Here we go. Flicking his one good eye up, he watched Quinn down her second glass of champagne. Their high metabolism made it hard to get anything other than the faintest buzz from alcohol, but it looked like she was going to do her best. Nikolas moved the bottle out of her reach, putting himself directly in the path of her wrath again. Troy shifted in his seat, unable to deal with the fucked-up dynamic between them.

Keeping his eyes down, Dutton began to speak. "One of my scouts returned this morning from Palmetto County." Where Nikolas acted as their father's protector, Dutton served as his eyes and ears. His spymaster controlling the information flowing across the sprawling state of Florida and beyond in a network covering the neighboring states. Not much happened that didn't make its way across Dutton's desk sooner or later.

"It appears a new pack has established themselves outside of Sarasota. They are small and very tight-knit. My scout had to leave before he drew too much suspicion, so my data about them is sketchy at best." He paused, giving Troy time to absorb the information.

Other packs existed in Florida and the surrounding states, but they all fell beneath the dubious shelter of the Brighton pack. Clark sat as reigning alpha over all them, demanding fealty and service, in both practical and financial terms. Every pack paid a quarterly tithe, and the strongest members were either killed or assimilated under Clark's direct control. Troy, Quinn, and the others had been forcibly removed from their own packs as children when Brighton overran them.

"They have established themselves in a community and look to be putting down roots," Dutton continued. "New businesses have opened, all run by members of the pack."

"And yet they have failed to approach me for permission," Clark snapped.

And there it is. If the new pack was small and inwardly focused, they might not even be aware of the existence of other packs in the state. Most wolf packs steered well clear of each other, keeping large neutral buffers between their territorial lands. Shifter packs traditionally followed the same strictures. Unless their alpha was a megalomaniac, like Clark.

"Troy." His father's sharp tone scattered his musings. Failure to pay attention at the alpha's table could get you in serious trouble. "You will go to this backwater town of...." Clark snapped his fingers at Dutton.

"Moonlight."

"You will go to Moonlight and explain to their

alpha the error of his ways. Take your time; I want to know everything about them." The alpha stopped, waiting for the submissives to clear their empty plates and serve the main course. A savory aroma rose from the steaming plate of shrimp, a particular favorite of Troy's. His stomach turned as the scent of the familiar spices hit his nose. Knowledge of what lay ahead destroyed his appetite. He'd trodden the same path before. Guilt weighed heavy, dropping his shoulders.

"It won't be easy," Dutton cautioned. "Samuel is one of my best scouts, and they closed ranks on him. He's played the lone wolf before and eased his way into other packs, but they moved him on within hours of him entering the local diner."

Forcing himself to eat the shrimp, Troy considered his options. Refusing to go was out of the question. He trusted Dutton's opinion. If one of his team couldn't infiltrate Moonlight, then a different tactic would be required. After draining the last of his champagne, he folded his napkin and placed it next to his empty plate. "I'll approach the alpha directly, offer him the hand of friendship." A glimmer of hope beckoned, and Troy held his tongue until he knew he could speak without revealing any hint of excitement. "A female would be useful to help break the ice. Would open doors more likely to be closed to a single male."

An indulgent chuckle from the alpha dragged him back to reality. Shaking his head, Clark fixed a hollow smile on Troy. "Ah, son. You know how hard it is for me to part from any of my children. I will feel your absence every day you are away from my side and will rely on our dear Quinn to keep me company." He held his hand out across the table toward Quinn, beckoning her to approach.

With a bitter twist of her lips, she rose from her seat, circling the table to assume her position at the alpha's left side, resting her hand on his shoulder. *Shit*. If it were only him, Troy would run as far and as fast as he could. He respected Dutton, tolerated Nikolas, but would leave them both without a backward glance if he could. They had nothing holding them to Clark's side other than their own fucked-up sense of loyalty.

An image of a five-year-old Quinn burying her tear-stained face into his lap taunted him. She may be all grown up and capable of defending herself, but Troy owed her an unrepayable debt. If he'd been quicker, smarter, braver, they wouldn't be in the mess they were now. The destruction of their pack was on him.

Chapter Two

Ｔhe familiar masculine scent of her alpha reached Belinda Thomas a moment before he knocked on the frame of her open door. His tall outline filled the doorway, cast in shadow by her screen door. Humidity lay thick in the air, a damp weight she could taste on the back of her tongue. The slightest movement sucked sweat from every pore. Her once-crisp white blouse clung to the base of her spine, and she'd shoved her hair back off her face with a glitter hairband more suited to a young teenager than a grown woman. Bel didn't care. Pretty things drew her like a magpie, and no outfit could be called complete without a glittery accent.

"Come on in, Derek," she said, turning toward the refrigerator to lift out a huge jug of iced tea. Drops of condensation formed on a pair of tall glasses the moment she filled them. She slid one across the counter toward him, raising her own to press it against her cheek. The cold kiss of the glass brought a modicum of relief from the oppressive heat.

Derek drained his drink in one long gulp, smiling in thanks when she poured him a second. "This heat is going to kill me," he grumbled, taking a more modest sip this time.

Strands of dark hair clung to his forehead, and she clenched her fist against the urge to brush them away. The alpha was happily mated now, and she had no touch rights anymore. Riesa suited him. Her insightful nature soothed and comforted Derek in a way Bel had never been able to. Had never wanted to, in truth. Wolves were highly sexual, and the unmated members of the pack relied on each other to serve their needs. Less aggressive than most, Bel had been fortunate when Derek took her into his bed, treating her with gentleness even if it didn't give him the levels of satisfaction his dominant nature craved. A good alpha understood each individual member of his pack and worked hard to deliver what they needed to be safe and secure. To be alpha meant to put all things before your own personal requirements.

She might miss his familiar weight between her thighs, but she knew Riesa and Derek were wholly devoted to each other. Her own loneliness seemed a small price to pay in the face of their happiness. There were available males in the pack, but few wanted to get close enough to Bel. Being omega of the pack gave her insights into the deepest reaches of those around her. She couldn't blame a casual lover for wanting to guard their secrets. Thanks to the ever-expanding range of sex toys available online, she could take the edge off her needs. She didn't lack for orgasms, but it would be nice to experience the scents and sounds of shared intimacy once in a while.

Derek growled low in his throat. "You're not happy, Bel. What can I do to help you?"

Shedding her little cloud of self-pity, she gave him a sunny smile. "I'm fine, Derek. It would be nice to be able to do a few chores around the place without needing to take a damn shower, but other than that...." Shrugging one shoulder, she dismissed his concern. "It's lovely to see you, Alpha, but I'm guessing this isn't a social call."

Derek frowned at her for a few moments more before he accepted her switching the topic of conversation. He wouldn't let it go for long, but she'd avoided the inevitable awkward talk for another day. "There's a new wolf in town."

Her head snapped up. Personal concerns took a backseat when it came to any potential threat to the pack. Given the struggles they'd been through to escape their old life, nothing was more important than peace and stability for their small group. Settling in Moonlight had offered a chance at normality after years of strife and pain. They would do whatever it took to protect it.

"Another one?" She folded her arms, resting her hips against the counter behind her. Derek wanted to expand the pack. A number of new members, including humans, now lived among them. Word went out that lone wolves had a place of safety here, provided they could make a positive contribution to the overall well-being of the pack. It meant more work for Bel, and not all the newcomers proved sincere in their motives. The last stranger who'd walked into the convenience store a few weeks before raised her hackles so high Bel had dropped her basket and sprinted the half mile to Kirk's remote cabin. The strongest wolf in their pack, Kirk was their first and last line of defense. His once fierce outer shell shattered now by a sweet, curvy human determined to draw the big wolf into the center of pack life. His utter capitulation in the face of Silver's love surprised many, but not Bel. She'd seen the gaping void in his soul, the noble truth in his heart regardless of the poor opinion he held about himself. Thankfully, he no longer avoided her like the plague, and his mate was becoming a great friend.

Kirk and Derek had escorted the stranger out of town, but she could still feel the echoes of his malevolence in her mind. And now, the alpha stood in the kitchen, needing her to test her ability against another unknown wolf. A shiver of foreboding sent goose bumps racing up her arms.

Derek raised an eyebrow. "This one is different. He's come as an emissary for another pack. Their territory is a couple of hours from here based in the Brighton Reservation."

She pressed a palm to her chest, trying to calm the sudden racing of her heart. Driven from their home by the encroachment of hunters and then the vicious attack of another pack which decimated their numbers, they'd settled in Moonlight after months of hiding in an abandoned orange grove. Plans to regroup and move on were put aside when Alexa joined the pack and brought with her the opportunity for the pack to settle in the rundown cottages they now called home. Quiet relief slowly replaced the constant pall of fear hanging over them. It would break her heart if they had to run again.

Derek closed the distance between them. She wasn't aware of the tears falling down her cheeks until they dripped from her chin. She longed to indulge her need for touch for a moment, but mated wolves couldn't tolerate the scent of another female on them. Settling for the next best thing, she reached out to him with her gift. His emotions were as familiar to her as her own. She sorted through the strands, soothing his tension and boosting his confidence.

"Don't tweak me, Bel," he growled, although there was no anger in his tone. "Moonlight is our home, and I'll do whatever it takes to defend it." He reached out, catching her pointed chin between his fingers to make her meet his gaze. "I need to hear what the Brighton pack wants from us, and I need you to be there. Can you do this for me?"

Her alpha needed her; the pack needed her. "Yes," she whispered, cleared her throat, and tried again. "Yes, Derek, I'll help in any way I can." She tucked her worries and fears away in a corner of her mind. If things went wrong, she would have plenty of time in the future to indulge them.

***

"Stop fiddling with your apron, you look fine."

Belinda blushed under Hannah's gentle admonishment. The pack second's mate worked in the Moonlight Diner part-time, and she'd agreed to an extra shift to guide Bel through the unfamiliar role. Derek had decided offering a meal to the emissary would present an impression of cooperation. By posing as a waitress, Bel could get close to their table without drawing attention to herself. People tended to overlook servers, treating them as part of the fixtures and fittings. Several members of the pack were scattered around the room, including Hannah's mate, Rand. He perched on a stool at the main counter a couple of feet from where they stood, sharing coffee and pie with Kirk. Between the two of them and Derek, any threat from the Brighton emissary would be neutralized in seconds.

"Hey, baby, you got something hot there for me?" Rand jiggled his coffee cup at Hannah, grinning at the blush rising on her cheeks.

"Give me a fucking break," Kirk rumbled from the other side of Rand. "You'd better get him a jug of ice water, put out the fire in his pants."

Bel snorted, clapping her hand over her mouth at the undignified noise. Rand laughed, the easy warm sound teasing more giggles from her. She turned her back on the room, trying and failing to stem them. Her shoulder's shook and tears sprang up in her eyes. The joke hadn't even been that funny, but it helped to break the bubbles of nervous tension in her stomach. Taking a few deep breaths, she settled herself, dabbing at her eyes with a napkin from the counter dispenser.

"Feeling better, Mix?" the second asked, and she nodded. He'd given her the nickname years ago, when she'd been trying to get to grips with her omega abilities. Rand had compared her to a mixing board, damping some emotions, amplifying others, helping members of the pack to find the perfect balance they needed to broadcast at optimum levels. It was a bit more complicated than that, but the analogy worked enough to help the rest of the pack understand what she could do.

The phone next to Rand's plate vibrated, and he glanced at the screen. "He's here."

Bel sobered in an instant. She picked up a couple of menus, put them back down, and fiddled with her apron again until Hannah gave the back of her hand a gentle slap.

"Relax, Bel," she murmured before moving away with the coffee pot to do a top-up round. The door to the diner opened, letting a sultry gust of air into the temperature-controlled atmosphere. The low evening sun dazzled through the open door, obscuring her view of the two men as they entered. Gathering the menus, she moved away from the counter toward the center of the room. The welcoming smile she directed at Derek froze on her lips when the man behind closed the door and turned toward her. She'd heard the term breathtaking, had used it herself before, but had never actually experienced it until that moment.

Derek had always turned her head with his dark hair and intense golden eyes. The stranger beside him looked lighter, brighter—the sun peeking out from behind Derek's dark cloud. His warm smile, shining green eyes, and relaxed demeanor drew her like a moth to a flame. She wanted to touch him, pet him, attract his attention in any way she could. A shudder rippled through her, and she folded her arms across her chest to disguise the sudden hardening of her nipples.

The alpha steered his guest toward the prearranged booth. The rest of the diners had been positioned to give an impression of privacy. With their enhanced shifter hearing, any conversation at the table above a whisper would carry to everyone present. Detailed discussions about the emissary's reason for visiting would not be held in public. This meal was for show and to give both parties the opportunity to size each other up.

Derek raised an eyebrow at her, and she tried to shake off her shocking reaction to the strange wolf. Licking her dry lips, she fixed her smile and approached the table. She had a job to do. The alpha needed her focused on the task he'd set her. *Hot damn, he smells incredible.* The sensitive flesh between her legs prickled in awareness. Fur tickled beneath her skin, and her wolf senses went on point. Something flashed through the visitor's eyes—an acknowledgment he schooled into friendly blankness.

"I'll take an ice tea please, Bel," Derek murmured. She dragged her eyes away from the emissary and focused on the alpha. He gave her a quizzical glance then switched his focus to his guest. "What would you like to drink, Troy?"

"Ice tea sounds perfect. I think I sweat a pint walking from the car to the front door." His voice stroked against her skin, like a brush of dark promise. She glanced at his perfectly crisp linen suit over a white button-down shirt. Not a strand of his sandy-brown hair lay out of place. He looked clean and fresh. She swayed closer to draw in another lungful of his eucalyptus scent. She wanted to climb in his lap and rub herself against him until she carried his tangy essence on every inch of her skin.

"Bel?" Derek closed his hand around her wrist, pulling her back to awareness.

She closed her eyes, concentrating on his familiar touch, grounding herself in pack. *Get a damn grip, Bel.* Nodding once, she placed the menus on the table. "I'll fetch those drinks for you, gentlemen."

Derek released her, and she forced herself to

walk slowly to the service point. The simple task of fixing the tea settled her further, and she took the time to examine her reaction to the man. *Troy.* Her visceral attraction to him had blinded her omega nature. Everything she'd taken from him was superficial, the easy smiling façade he'd presented. She hadn't felt this out of control for years. Meditation had helped her through the roller coaster of puberty when the roil of teen hormones sent her haywire. Thankfully, the mental exercises came to her the moment she reached for them, and she guided herself through each step. She scooped ice, mixed the tea, and arranged a selection of citrus slices and individual sweetener packets on a plate, making each motion a mindful act.

By the time she carried the laden tray back to the booth, she had regained her equilibrium. The two men chatted, exchanging superficial information. They paused to thank her when she served their drinks before returning to their conversation. She moved into the background, drawing a notepad and pen out of the front pocket in her apron.

"And is your sister older or younger than you?" Derek asked, tipping the contents of two packets of sweetener into his glass. He stirred the dark liquid, added several orange slices, and took a sip.

"Younger." Troy fixed his tea to his own taste, giving Bel the chance to study him. A confusing mix of pride, worry, and distress swirled around him. He shielded well. His easy body language and open countenance would fool anyone other than an omega like her. Settling back into the well-worn leather of his seat, he lifted his menu to study it. "So how long have you been in Moonlight?"

19

The deliberate casualness of his question sent her mental alarm bells ringing. The cloud of emotions around him vanished, swallowed by a sense of all-encompassing determination. The force of it struck her like a physical blow. Bel dropped her pen, giving herself the chance to crouch down and disguise the sudden weakness in her knees. Her heart fluttered beneath her rib cage like a trapped bird as her fight-or-flight instincts kicked in. The tips of her fingers itched, and the bones of her jaw rippled.

Fighting the urge to shift, Bel grabbed frantically for her control exercises. She fumbled the pen, knocking it under a nearby table, and dived after it. Pressing her palms into the cool tiled floor, she focused on the physical sensations of her body. The brush of her hair against the nape of her neck, the way her tennis shoes pinched her bent toes, the painful dig of her underwired bra into the side of her breast. A chair scraped back, and the scents of eucalyptus and clean sweat filled her nose. She tilted her head, peering through her bangs into Troy's warm green eyes. The dangerous threat he posed to the pack she'd sensed moments before had vanished. Loyalty, honor, and a fierce desire to live in peace among them all resonated from him.

"Everything okay, miss?" he asked with a smile that warmed her cheeks.

Waving her pen under his nose, she plastered a smile on her face. "Found it!"

Crawling back on her hands and knees, she brushed a crease from her skirt and tried to make sense of everything. Troy had the potential to destroy their pack or become one of its greatest assets. She needed to figure out which path he would take. And soon.

Chapter Three

His move to follow her beneath the table had been driven entirely by instinct. From the moment he'd laid eyes on the pretty blonde, he'd been mesmerized. She looked wholesome and cute in her trim uniform, from the candy-striped ankle socks to the sparkly barrettes in her hair. His wolf howled in his skull, the noise drowning out everything, including the thumping pulse of his heated blood. Like everyone else present, she was a wolf shifter, but she had an otherworldly air about her he found fascinating. The way her cornflower-blue eyes widened every time they rested on him sent his cock into overdrive. He wanted to lap her up, wanted to curl around her and soak up the sweetness he saw in her smile. Pushing to his feet, Troy slid quickly into the booth, grateful the single-breasted jacket of his lightweight suit covered the front of his body to the top of his thighs.

Derek stared at him in full alpha mode. The burn of power in his golden irises hit Troy and he lowered his head. He needed to get control, and fast. The man in front of him didn't seem likely to miss much, and if he suspected Troy was interested in one of the females of his pack? He clenched his fist in his lap to hide a tremor of fear. He was acting like an amateur, giving the alpha the perfect excuse to remove him from the vicinity before they even opened discussions.

"We keep things simple here," the alpha said, eyes flicking between Troy's suit and his own much-more casual shirt and jeans. "I can recommend everything on the menu, though. Just make sure you leave room for a slice of key lime pie."

Grasping onto the resumption of conversation with grateful hands, Troy plied his whole attention to the menu in front of him. Bel had moved away to clear a table on the other side of the diner, which helped him regain his focus. The menu choices might be simple, but the cooking smells drifting from the kitchen set his mouth watering.

"Simple sounds good," he said, only realizing how true that was as he said the words. Having shrugged off his jacket, he rolled the sleeves of his white shirt to the elbow. After the chicanery of home, simple sounded fucking fantastic. The tension he'd carried for the past two weeks since his father's assault eased, and his shoulders dropped a couple of inches. A soft squeak of tennis shoes on tile warned him of Bel's approach.

"Are you ready?"

He watched the easy interaction between Derek and Bel, a familiarity and light teasing he didn't think he'd ever shared with a woman. Troy took great pains to keep a distance between himself and the few partners he took to bed. Their interactions were mutually satisfying, but he chose carefully to ensure he didn't share an intimacy with anyone who might get ideas about dating the son of their alpha on a regular basis. His loneliness mattered little in comparison to keeping them off Clark's radar. He would not willingly place another weapon in his father's sick armory. Suppressing a tinge of envy, he basked in the smile Bel turned upon him. Gentle, sweet, a little clumsy—everything about her appealed to him. His wolf perked up. If he gave his animal side its way, he'd be begging at her feet for a pat on the head. The little witch had him mesmerized.

"I'd like a cheeseburger and side salad please, Bel." Her pen paused a heartbeat or two at his use of her name, giving him a surge of satisfaction. Whatever relationship she had with the alpha, this pretty little wolf liked him.

She cut her gaze to him. "Anything else?" God damn it, the knowing glint in her eyes slayed him.

Take me, use me, cut my heart out with a dull spoon. "Not right now, maybe later."

His burger was cooked to perfection, still a little pink in the center and melt-in-the-mouth juicy. Troy closed his eyes in brief appreciation as he savored the meal. When was the last time he'd sat in the presence of an alpha and been able to enjoy his food? Derek carried the leadership of his pack with easy confidence. He didn't give the impression he required the bowing and scraping deference so many required, his father included. The talk between them shifted from sports, to the latest television series that seemed to have gripped most of the nation. When it moved to state politics, the alpha paid closer attention, asking pointed questions to mine Troy's local knowledge. They talked around the purpose of his visit, avoiding

anything shifter-related, but one thing was clear—
Derek and his pack had put down roots and looked
set to stay. *Damn.*

Regret washed through him. Here was an alpha
he would follow given half a chance. Every passing
moment widened the gulf between the pack he'd been
raised in and the tight-knit group who had settled in
Moonlight. Over the course of their meal, the various
shifters in the room dropped past their table and
shared a few words with the alpha. He welcomed
them all with equal enthusiasm regardless of their
level of dominance. It didn't escape Troy's notice they
all gravitated toward Bel as well. Her sunny smile
never wavered. The skin at the back of his neck itched
with the need to have her pet him the way she
touched her pack mates. Each person left her
presence in a bright mood, even the hulking guy at
the counter who cast an evil eye toward Troy every
couple of minutes. The pressurized atmosphere in the
room lifted in increments until a collective sigh
echoed around the room. The wolves around him
were no longer on highest alert. Even the alpha
appeared inclined to give him a chance. He didn't
know how she'd done it, but Bel had given him a foot
in the door. He could move around these people, get
to know them a little. They would be suspicious, of
course, but he doubted they'd slam doors in his face.

"If you're going to stick around for a few days, I
need you to stay in town. We have a guest cottage you
can use." Derek slid his plate to the side and rested
his folded arms on the table in front of him. His body
language must have been a prearranged cue because
the two men from the counter moved immediately to
the side of the booth. The bigger of the two glowered

at him. The thick, white scar bisecting his dark beard pulled tight in time with the muscle tic in his jaw.

Derek pushed to his feet. "Kirk and Rand will escort you to your hotel to gather your things. I'll also require you to hand over your electronic devices."

Troy nodded once; he'd expected nothing less. Lifting his folded jacket from the seat next to him, he pulled his car keys from the pocket and placed them on the table. The big man scooped them up, handing them off to a third man clad in gray overalls, who ghosted over.

"Thanks, Knox," the alpha murmured.

"No problem." He flashed a quick grin toward Troy. "I'll take care of your baby, don't worry."

Troy cast a worried look after the departing man, and Kirk clapped him on the shoulder. "Knox is cool. He runs the local garage here in Moonlight. You'll get your car back in one piece." The big man gave him an evil grin. "Or mostly one piece."

***

Soft rain pattered on the overhanging roof. Troy sank into the padded wicker chair on the back porch of the single-story cottage, a cold beer sweating in his hand. The rain thickened the hot air further, making it hard to breath. Moisture already darkened the waistband of the sweat shorts he'd pulled on after his shower. He'd eschewed a T-shirt, unable to face anything else confining his skin. Kirk and Rand had been respectful in their treatment, but his wolf chafed hard over the violation of his personal property. They'd searched his bags, confiscating his phone, laptop, even his e-reader. They'd dropped him at the cottage an hour before, leaving explicit instructions for him not to leave without the escort who would show him around the town in the morning.

The rear of the building faced a wooded area, and he doubted anyone who saw him would be concerned at his state of dress. Nudity was accepted among shifters. The thick tree line tempted him. A run would settle both man and wolf enough he might be able to snatch a few hours' sleep. He raised the beer to his lips, draining half the contents. Running in another pack's territory without an explicit invitation would be a serious violation. Regardless of how uncomfortable his wolf might be, Troy did not want to risk pissing off the Moonlight alpha. There had to be a way to play both sides of this terrible situation and find a way out for him and Quinn. *There has to be.*

Wood creaked to his left, and Troy stilled, lowering his feet down from the porch railing. The heavy shadow of the overhang would conceal his presence. Rand had made a point of telling him he shared the home to the right with his mate but hadn't mentioned the occupant of the cottage on the opposite side. A pale reflection caught his eye, moonlight shining on light hair. The slender figure moving toward the woods paused and glanced in his direction. *Bel.*

He was out of his chair before realizing he'd moved; the thick railing around the porch was all that prevented him from striding across the open space toward her. Rain pattered against his skin, mixing with the sheen of sweat coating his chest. If she had turned away, kept moving without acknowledging him, he might not have acted. But he'd never know.

Instead, she raised a hand to her throat, drawing his eye to the delicate line of her arm, the expanse of bare skin above the low neckline of her simple dress.

Bending his knees, Troy leaped onto the railing, balancing on his toes in a crouch. She turned her head, glanced toward the woods then back in his direction. The last vestiges of the mask of civility he wore slipped away, and he bared his teeth in a feral grin. *Do it,* he urged silently.

As though she heard his voiceless plea, Bel spun on her heel and made a break for the trees. Growling low in his throat, he sprang from the railing, hitting the ground at full speed. The clouds overhead burst open, turning the gentle patter of rain into a raging torrent, soaking him to the skin in moments. His feet slipped and slid in the long grass underfoot, but he didn't slow his pace. Diving between a pair of thick trunks, he ducked beneath long curtains of Spanish moss and passed instantly into full darkness. The tangled canopy overhead masked the worst of the rain. Twigs snapped, warning her of his approach, marking her own desperate flight through the woods. Her scent hung thick in the humid air, a blanket of sunshine and sweetbriar.

A twisted root caught his ankle, sending him sprawling forward. Tucking his shoulder, he rolled with the motion, gaining his footing moments later at the base of a small incline. He stood in the bottom of a natural hollow, a clearing in the trees. Bel was less than twenty feet away, clutching the skirt of her dress high as she scrambled up the other side of the hollow.

"Stop," he growled, forcing every ounce of command he possessed into the word.

She froze, one foot on the crest of the slope. He

stalked across the clearing, watching her shoulders heave as she tried to catch her breath. He knew how she felt. Between the thick summer air and the lust coursing through his veins, he might never breathe normally again. The muscles in her calf twitched where her toes braced for purchase on the incline. He'd never spent much time considering the graceful shape of the back of a woman's leg before. The curve of muscle narrowing to taper into the rigidity of an Achilles tendon, the pregnant swell of a smooth heel, the arch of her elegant instep.

Pausing at the base of the slight hill, he reached for her leg, traced the lean muscle of her calf. He slid his hand higher, watching it disappear beneath the damp hem of her dress. A soft gasp escaped her lips. Bending his head, he nibbled along the defined edge of her calf muscle, burying his lips into the dimple at the back of her knee.

"Troy!" His name on her lips sounded both a blessing and a curse. Keeping his hand clamped around the back of her thigh, he pushed himself up the slope, forcing her forward until they both stood fully on flat ground. The twisted trunk of a huge oak blocked their path a few feet in front of them.

"Brace your hands on the tree," he murmured, releasing his grip on her slick skin. She stepped forward, moving without hesitation, which pleased him no end. He closed the small distance between them, leaving bare inches between her back and the front of his body. His cock strained beneath the soft jersey material of his shorts, eager to brush against the ripeness of her ass. He jerked her dress up in a swift motion, making her gasp again as he pulled it over her head and down her arms. He twisted the wet cotton, tangling it around her wrists, effectively binding her hands together where they rested against the rough bark of the tree. Its thick branches, and the cloud-covered skies, left him reliant on his wolf-enhanced eyesight. Her silhouette tapered from her strong shoulders into a trim waist, flowing out at the lush curve of her hips. It reminded him of Nikolas's cello. The delicate instrument looked ludicrous in his brother's huge grip, and yet he could coax the most beautiful music from its strings.

Troy licked his lips. He wanted to pluck and stroke Bel the same way until her voice sobbed and soared to a tune entirely of his making. He pressed his thumb between her shoulder blades, dragging it in one slow, firm motion down her spine until it rested at the very top of the seam of her ass. She arched her spine, pushing back into the digit, inviting him to slide lower. The bloom of arousal added a spicy tang to her sweet, natural fragrance. Resisting the urge to drop to his knees and bury his face between her legs, he raised his other hand, shifting both until he cupped her hips. He pulled her lower body backward, nudging her ankles farther apart until she bent over, her back at a thirty-degree angle to the trunk, head lowered between her shoulders. He traced the ebb and flow of her shape, gliding over her delicate curves, feeling her skin shiver beneath his fingers. Spreading his hands wide, he curled them around her rib cage, pausing when they brushed the underside of her firm breasts.

He stepped between her legs, letting her feel the weight of him against her back, nudging his rigid cock against her ass. The heat radiating from her skin scorched him through the material of his shorts, sending a hiss of breath between his clenched teeth. "Beautiful." He groaned against her ear. "You're so fucking beautiful, Bel." He caught the top of her shoulder between his teeth and bit down, loving the eager sob she made in response.

Duty dug its vicious claws into him, raking his guts, forcing the haze of his lust to recede. They shouldn't be doing this. Touching her risked everything. The wrath of her alpha. The fury of his father if Derek sent him away before his mission had even started. The threat to Quinn if he failed to find a way to get them both out of the clutches of the Brighton pack. Bel must feel it, too, must know letting an almost stranger touch her could pose a danger to herself and her pack.

"Tell me no, Bel," he begged against the damp hair clinging to the nape of her neck. "Tell me this is madness, and somehow I'll find the strength to turn and walk away."

"I can't," she said, voice full of regret and longing. "I don't care about what's right and what's wrong. I just need you to keep touching me." Her hips rocked back, notching his cloth-covered erection in the vee at the top of her thighs. He snarled, shifting his hands until they cupped her breasts, capturing the hard peaks of her nipples between his fingers. Pinching the tender flesh, he twisted and tugged, unable to find the gentleness she deserved in the red blaze of lust engulfing him. His wolf rose, driving his need higher, and his humanity fell away. The calm reasonable man he presented to the world vanished, replaced by a being of the basest instincts and wants.

Chapter Four

Sanity, reason, control. They were all strangers to her as Bel writhed and gasped beneath his fierce touch. Every pinch, every stroke sent waves of heat coursing through her body, arrowing to the center of her being. She could taste his lust for her on her tongue, ripe, heady, the rich wash of eucalyptus sending her head spinning. No one had touched her like this, not even Derek. Always so careful of her omega nature, her previous lovers had petted and coaxed, but never demanded. Troy demanded everything. Touched her like he wanted to own her, break her down to a molecular level, and build her again into a creature of pure need. She wanted it, too. More than anything.

Thrusting her hips back, she ground against the rigid heat of his cock, needing it. Needing him to fill her to overflowing and beyond. Blood rose to the surface of her skin. She could hear the incessant beat of rain on the canopy overhead. Wished she could feel it on her heated flesh. Something, anything to lessen the burn.

He twisted her nipples again, a sharp pinch,

followed immediately by a softer stroke. The contrast drove her wild, and she thought she could come from the touch of his hands on her breasts alone. Who knew she would love this? Who even suspected a dark desire lurked within her soul, a need, a pulse so violent she wanted to throw back her head and scream to the heavens.

He knew.

Desperate mewls filled the air, choking from her own throat. "Troy. Please. Now. Need you." The ability to form a coherent sentence deserted her.

The wolf within rose. Stretching, luxuriating in the demanding touch of this man, this stranger, this *mate?*

Harsh fingers plucked again, shaping and kneading her flesh, driving the fleeting thought away on a fresh wave of desire. She shifted her feet, wanting to close her legs and press her thighs together against the aching throb deep in her sex. The sharp edge of his teeth glanced across her shoulder. A growl rumbled in his throat, stilling her instantly. He changed his grip, spanning one hand across both her breasts, sliding the other down over the slight curve of her belly to cup her sex.

The weight of his fingers resting against the seam of her pussy sent a whimper from her throat and she rolled her hips. If she found just the right angle, she could work the tip of his middle finger between her lips, find the relief her clit craved. He locked his hand, thwarting her efforts, changing her whimpers to a growl of frustration. A deep chuckle rumbled against her back, rippling down her spine.

"What's the matter, *ma belle*? Do you ache for me? Do you hunger for my touch the way I hunger for yours?" His accent slowed, thickened into a deeper drawl.

Yes. Yes. So hungry. Starving for him as though deprived of the essential nutrients needed to sustain her very existence. "Troy." She groaned, clawing at the rough bark of the tree beneath her fingers.

"I've got you, *ma belle.* I've got just what you need, baby," he crooned, curling his fingers to breach her seam. The first stroke against her clit sent her screaming over the edge, but he didn't stop there. Gliding through the soaking wetness of her pussy, he pressed the tips of his fingers against her opening, testing the tight ring of muscles. She shuddered, half-terrified, half-eager he might force her take the full width of them in one thrust. Moving farther back, he carried her slick arousal over her perineum to toy with the entrance to her ass.

"I don't. We can't. I haven't...."

He teased the very tip of one digit against her anus, and she held her breath, not sure what she wanted him to do next. This was far outside her sphere of sexual reference, skirting the edges of her wickedest fantasies. Fantasy didn't always make for a pleasant reality, though, and she huffed in relief when his fingers returned to her clit.

"I can't trust myself with you like that, *ma belle.* Not tonight," he muttered, dropping to his knees behind her. His hot breath panted against the top of her thighs, teasing her sensitive flesh. Raising her right leg, he rested her knee on his shoulder, bracing his hands on the ground to take her weight. She lowered her head farther, looking between her breasts. Her body obscured the upper part of his face, but she watched in fascination as his tongue curled out to rub her clit.

The combination of physical and visual stimuli ramped her desire. His chin glistened wetly, coated in her arousal. She'd always been a lights-off, covers-pulled-up kind of girl before. No more, though. She rocked her hips into his face, earning a growl of approval and a deeper stroke of his tongue. He moved his mouth, stiffening his tongue to fuck it in and out of her pussy, and his fingers clenched, digging into the soil beneath his hands. Her fingers curled, too, pressing into the tree trunk, shredding her tender skin, but she was too far gone to care about the tiny hurt. Sitting back suddenly on his thighs, Troy grabbed her around her waist, tugging her down to straddle his lap. His hands grasped hers, dragging her abused fingertips to his lips. He sucked gently, plying the scrapes with his tongue to lap away the sting. The tangle of her dress still bound her wrists, and he unwrapped it, shaking out the thin cotton to lay it on the ground in front of them.

Easing her from his lap, he turned her until she stared up at him. He stood in one fluid motion, towering over her splayed form. She felt vulnerable, like prey before a fierce predator. A fresh burst of arousal dampened the top of her thighs. With one hard jerk, he removed his shorts, then folded the thick material in a long strip and knelt between her legs. He tucked the soft jersey beneath her elbows, cushioning her against the hard ground. Only the rapid rise and fall of his chest gave any indication he was in less than perfect control. He cupped her left breast, drawing it up toward his lowering mouth, capturing the entirety of its small circumference. He sucked hard, notching her nipple against the roof of his mouth. The heavy weight of his cock pressed into the top of her mound, and she cried out his name. She wanted him inside her. Needed to connect their bodies in the most fundamental way.

This was what she had been created for. To be a vessel for their combined passion, the crucible to contain and consume their burning lust. Fumbling between their bodies, she captured his silken flesh, guiding the head of his cock to the entrance of her body. She thrust her hips, taking the first inches of him inside her. His teeth dug into her breast, a brief convulsion before he released her on a guttural cry. Gripping her hips, he took control, settling back on his haunches to drag her lower body up his thighs. With infuriating slowness, he fed his cock into her body in steady increments. Braced on her elbows, she had a clear view of everything. Could watch as he slid in and out of her core. Head lowered, he, too, watched the mating of their flesh. The slabbed muscles of his abdomen rippled with each motion of his hips, and she licked her lips. Power and control, strength and grace—this magnificent creature was all hers.

"You feel so good, *ma belle*. So fucking hot and wet I want to fuck you forever." He dug his fingers into her thighs, increasing the pace of his thrusts as sweat dripped from his forehead to land with a splash on the curve of her belly. He added a roll to his forward motion, finding the perfect spot deep inside her. She closed her eyes, unable to handle the overload of sensations wracking her body. A myriad of scents and sounds battered her senses. The zingy freshness of his eucalyptus, her own heady sweetbriar. Sweat, musk, the deep green of the woods, the earthiness of the soil churned up beneath their bodies. Soft pants, hard grunts, the slick and slap of flesh meeting and parting. There was no Bel, no Troy. There was only the point connecting them, melding them into a single grasping, yearning entity.

"More, need more," he growled, pressing forward to cover her body with his. Gripping her by the shoulder and thigh, he drove harder against her with every stroke. She lifted her legs, hooking her ankles at the base of his spine, creating the perfect angle to take him deeper still. A coil wound in her belly, tighter and tighter until she feared she would snap from the pressure.

"Too much, too much!" Her head thrashed from side to side, and she didn't know if she was trying to get away from him or press closer.

"Never, Bel. Never enough. I need this, need you to take it. Take everything I have, baby." He faltered above her, teeth biting into his lip until she could scent the blood he drew. It was the final key to the puzzle, the final stimulant she needed, and her wolf howled in triumph as she lunged forward to drag his lower lip into her mouth. Blood welled from the injury, flooding her mouth as his hot seed filled her pussy, and she flew apart, lost to everything but the taste of him.

Something bumped her hip, and she swam up through the darkness in time to feel the heavy weight of Troy's body jerk away from her.

"Motherfucker! Look at what you've done to her. There's blood on her mouth, you bastard!" The murderous fury in Kirk's voice chased away the last of her stupor, and she touched her hand to her lips.

"It's not my blood, Kirk."

She stared up at the men encircling her. Derek and Rand stood on one side; Troy struggled in Kirk's hold on the other.

"Stop looking at her," Troy snarled, his wolf shining bright in his eyes.

Her pack mates looked rumpled, confused, and angry. Derek's black hair tumbled across his forehead, and a thick red mark stood out against the bare skin of his chest. Rand looked dazed, clad in only a pair of jeans he'd half-fastened. A set of livid claw marks ran down one arm.

Bel reached for them, seeking to soothe the distress filling the clearing, but she came up empty. She could sense them, could feel the roil of emotions, but it felt like she was encased in amber, separated from her pack by a translucent shield. "What happened?" she asked, although she had a pretty good idea. Tucking her knees up, she curled her arms around them in a protective ball.

Troy roared a sound of incoherent fury and broke away from Kirk, diving to his knees to gather her close against his chest. Exhaustion settled deep inside her limbs, and she turned her face, seeking the warm safety of the curve of his throat. Drawing deep breaths, she used his already-familiar scent to calm her racing mind.

"You projected, Bel," Derek said, confirming her worst fears. It hadn't happened for years. Not since she was a teenager struggling to come to terms with her emotional connection to the pack.

"How bad?" she whispered, burrowing nearer to the solid warmth of Troy's body.

"Depends on your definition of bad," Rand replied. "If you don't mind the whole pack knowing you got your world rocked by Mr. Smooth here, then not bad at all." The hint of humor in his voice offered a slight balm to the surge of embarrassed horror coursing through her.

"Everyone?"

"Mrs. Meyer sounded very happy when I ran past their place on the way here," Kirk muttered. "And Silver punched me in the face."

Oh. God.

Mrs. Meyer was eighty if she was a day, and the idea of Kirk's sweet, human mate striking him didn't bear thinking about.

"I'm so sorry, Kirk. Is she okay?"

The big man barked a laugh. "She's fine, just mad because I left our bed when she wanted to go again."

Humiliation burned through her, and she pressed her face deeper into Troy's shoulder.

"Belinda. Look at me." She raised her head, obeying the command of her alpha without hesitation. Derek lowered to one knee, ignoring the man beside her, focusing only on Bel. "Are you all right? Did you flame out?" It was a term they'd come up with when she overexerted her emotional abilities.

"I think so. I feel numb. Tired mostly, and more than a little embarrassed."

Troy brushed his lips across the top of her head, drawing her away when Derek reached out to touch her cheek.

The alpha snarled. "You need to tread very carefully. She's still mine, Troy. You disobeyed a direct order, and I am within my rights to remove you from our lands for this." His tone softened when she gasped in protest. Sitting back on his heels, he regarded them both. "Now is not the time to discuss this. Kirk isn't the only one with a disgruntled mate who needs soothing."

He rose to his feet, all supple strength and power. "Take her home, and then you will return to your own cottage." He silenced the rumble of protest from Troy with a slash of his hand. "No! You have already put my omega at risk with your selfish desires. We will talk more about this in the morning." Turning on his heel, the alpha stalked off, the other two wolves at his heels.

The bubble of tension in the clearing burst at their departure, leaving Bel bone tired. She stood when Troy urged her up, lifted her arms to let him slip her damp dress over her body. He dragged on his shorts and took her hand. After a few stumbling steps, he swung her up into his arms and strode through the woods. She didn't have the energy to protest, didn't even have the energy to speak, though she knew he must have questions. He didn't hesitate at her door. Using one elbow, he nudged the handle down then carried her through the kitchen and straight down the hallway to her bathroom. She pondered his seeming familiarity with the place before her sluggish brain remembered her home was a mirror image of the guest cottage next door. Lowering her onto the marble counter beside the sink, he fiddled with the shower until he found a satisfactory temperature setting. With a pat on her bottom, her removed her shift and nudged her into the shower. "I'll go and make you a drink. Are you hungry?"

She shook her head, letting the heat of the shower rinse away the sweat and dirt from her skin.

Washing her hair involved too much effort, so she settled for a half-hearted scrub of her hands through it to loosen any twigs. A few swipes of the soap, taking care with the tender ache between her thighs, and she shut the water off. He was there before she'd taken a full step out of the stall, enveloping her in a thick towel to dry her body. The quilt had already been turned back, and she slid gratefully into bed. Troy tucked the pillows around her, then placed a mug of tea in her hands.

"You don't have to go," she said, not sure she could bear to be parted from him even for a few hours. Her emotions might be scattered to the four winds, but she knew without a doubt the man before her was her mate. A flicker of doubt tightened the corner of his eyes, chased away moments later by a warm smile. Her heart sank. The charming mask he'd worn when she first saw him slid back in place.

"Derek would have my hide, and he'd be perfectly entitled to it. Get some sleep and we'll talk in the morning." He brushed a kiss against her cheek and left her alone.

She sipped her tea, ignoring the burn of the too-hot liquid on her tongue. Troy hadn't left her because he feared her alpha. Numb as she might be, she couldn't mistake the raw fear in his scent. She could pinpoint the moment it started. Protectiveness, possessiveness, and lingering desire had blazed from his every pore right up until Derek revealed her secret nature. Troy was scared of her being an omega.

Chapter Five

T roy stopped his incessant pacing to open the front door, sighing in resignation at the sight of one very pissed-off alpha on his doorstep. He hadn't slept a wink. Between the oppressive heat and his whirling brain, staying still in bed long enough to drop off had proven impossible. Omega. The word taunted him, pulsed in his head in time with the headache building behind his left eye. He moved away from the door, making sure not to turn his back on Derek and risk offering any further insult to the man. He'd enjoyed the conversation between them yesterday, had looked forward to learning more about the man behind the small, but loyal, pack hiding away in this little town.

"Can I offer you a drink?" His brain felt like it was packed with cotton wool, and he hoped going through the motions of politeness would give him time to find the right words to argue his case. He'd considered and dismissed so many possibilities during the pre-dawn hours he no longer had any idea what he wanted.

"Anything cold is fine." Derek strode into the

room, taking instant command of the space, as was his right. He walked through the house and straight out the back door where he settled on one of the two wicker chairs on the rear porch.

The sun wouldn't reach the area until early afternoon, so the shade offered some relief to the growing heat of the day. Troy joined him, offering a pair of sodas and popping open the one he was left with after Derek made his selection.

"Sit."

Doing as instructed, Troy took the empty chair, placing his drink between his bare feet. Hoping to blend in better on the off chance he was permitted to stay, he'd opted for a pair of beige cargo shorts and a plain T-shirt. He felt surprisingly vulnerable without the armor afforded by his usual suit, but the time for pretense was over. His one shot was to be as honest as he could without betraying his own pack and risking the future of Moonlight. Walking a tightrope strung with razor blades across the Grand Canyon might prove an easier feat, but he had no choice. Lives depended on what happened in the next few minutes, least of all his own.

Derek propped his can on the arm of his chair and tapped one nail against the cold metal. "You didn't know, did you?"

Troy closed his eyes for a brief second against the remembered image of Bel pausing to look at him before she ran for the trees. "It was a mistake. I can only offer my apologies to you for betraying your trust, together with my assurance it won't happen again." His wolf snarled in his head, furious to hear his human half deny the woman it craved. It didn't matter what the wolf wanted, or the man for that matter. She could not be theirs, so best to nip it in the bud. An omega would be too vulnerable among the dark horrors of the Brighton pack.

"And Bel agrees with you, about last night being a mistake?" The expression on the alpha's face matched his skeptical tone.

Leaning forward to pick up his drink, Troy twisted and turned it between his hands. "I thought you would be pleased. You were clearly unhappy last night."

"You took advantage of one of the most precious members of my pack, fucked her in the dirt like an animal, so *unhappy* is putting it mildly." A warning growl rumbled in Derek's chest, setting the hairs on the back of Troy's neck prickling.

He opened his mouth ready to protest. What had happened between him and Bel had been primal, earthy, driven entirely by instinct, but it had been way more than a dirty fuck. Which scared him half to death.

"You still didn't answer my question." Sliding farther down into his chair, the alpha rested his right foot on his left knee, looking completely at ease. "I don't have time to waste on what might have been and if-onlys, so we need to address the facts. You and Bel had sex and she lost control of herself in a way she hasn't in years, and never before in an intimate situation."

The certainty in Derek's voice raised his hackles, and a wash of furious jealousy turned his vision red. His fingers crushed the can of soda, sending cola spurting across his legs and feet. *Shit!* He was better at playing the game than this. Hadn't he learned from a harder man than Derek exactly how foolish it was to betray his emotions? Dragging in a deep breath, he held it for a count of five, blowing out the anger and tension in a long, ragged exhalation.

"Seems like she wasn't the only one who lost their control."

Troy ducked his head, avoiding the knowing look in Derek's eyes.

The alpha drained his drink, set the empty can beside his chair, and stood, folding his arms across his chest. "Why are you here, Troy?"

Christ, the man had a whole sack full of blindsiding questions. Shaking himself back into his role as pack emissary, he forced a smile to his lips. "I'm here to extend a hand of friendship from Brighton to Moonlight in the hope of fostering a mutually satisfying sense of cooperation between our packs."

Derek laughed, a harsh, bitter bark of sound. "Bullshit. I've got stuff to do. Come and see me when you are ready to stop lying to us both." Placing one hand on the porch railing, the alpha vaulted over it to land in the grass below.

"What about Bel?" The words were past Troy's lips before he could stop them.

"You can't stuff that genie back in the bottle, no matter how much you might want to. Bel's welfare is all I care about. First, last, always. If she wants to be with you, then you'd better man-the-fuck up and do what's right by her. I don't give a shit who your daddy is or how big your pack is; whatever happens between the two of you, she stays in Moonlight."

Craning his neck, he watched Derek lope across the open space to the cottage next door and disappear through the back door after a perfunctory knock. It should be him. He should have been the one knocking on her door, checking to make sure she was okay after last night. Shaking his head in self-disgust, he collected the empty drink cans and tossed them in the kitchen trash. The spilled soda had dried in a sticky mess on his legs. He needed a shower and a change of clothes. Hiding away in the cottage might be a fine idea, but he had work to do. Though his personal life was FUBAR, it would have to wait.

His hair still lay damp against his neck when another knock at his door came. The brief flash of hope it might be Bel faded when he tested the air, not catching her delicate sweetbriar scent. The alpha's second, Rand, stood on the doorstep, twirling one arm of a pair of sunglasses. He took one look at Troy's face and grinned.

"Sorry, man. I'm your date for the day." Clapping him on the shoulder, the second donned his shades and steered Troy out the door. "Derek wants me to show you around the place, explain a bit about how things work around here, and, in return, you can tell me a bit more about the deal you hope to broker between our packs."

Rand's words surprised him. Hadn't Derek called bullshit on his mission not ten minutes before? Whatever, he wouldn't look this gift wolf in the mouth. He would need to report back to Clark in the next few days, and his father would demand some intelligence about the local setup. With any luck, he might persuade the old man their latest target was too small a prize to bother about. Another lie. Jesus, he needed to get his head straight and start untangling the mess in his brain before he fucked up and got someone killed.

They spent the next couple of hours strolling around the town, stopping in at the various local businesses and homes. Rand knew everyone, knew exactly what was going on in their lives and had a word of advice, admiration, or consolation for each situation. Yes, this pack was significantly smaller than Brighton, but his father was so far removed from the people under his control he probably didn't know half their names. Troy knew most everybody in the pack; it was his job to connect with them all, even the outlying subpacks who bowed to Clark, but he didn't know their individual stories. The only person he could think of who probably did know would be Dutton. With his network of contacts, nothing happened within the confines of Brighton without his brother hearing about it. He doubted Dutton shared even a fraction of the information he gathered with Clark. In his own way, he managed the alpha better than any of them.

"So what does your father do?" Rand asked, as they exited the diner clutching a pair of iced coffees.

"Do? He runs the pack; he's the alpha."

"Yeah, yeah, he's the alpha, but what does he do for work? What business is he in? Derek and I run a security consultancy." Rand squatted down on the diner steps, taking advantage of the shade from the bright awning shielding the front window from the worst of the midday sun.

"Running the pack is a full-time job." Troy sank down beside Rand and sipped his drink thoughtfully. "Well, Dut, Nik, and I take care of most of the day-to-day stuff." What exactly did his father contribute to the pack? He brought a sense of control, garnered by fear rather than respect. He relied on those beneath to support him financially, taking a tithe from every family in return for his supposed protection. The sheer size of Brighton deterred other shifters from attacking them, but how much threat had they actually faced before Clark began his own ambitious expansion plans? He didn't seek to unite the wolves in the region for security; he sought power and wealth.

How many packs like Moonlight would have lived in peace and relative obscurity if Clark hadn't actively sought them out? He hadn't met a single person today who longed for anything other than peace and prosperity for themselves and their friends and families. A battered truck pulled up in front of the diner, disgorging a pair of sweating, smiling human males. Both wore weapons strapped to their belts and moved with the kind of strength and dominance few humans could. Troy shot to his feet in an instant, surprised when Rand continued to lounge upon the steps.

"Hey guys, what's up?" Rand said, offering his hand to each in turn.

"Hey, Rand," said the smiling dark-haired man who'd exited the driver's seat. "We've got a new case. Could use your input if you have time?"

The blond beside him stopped at the base of the steps directly below Troy and fixed his hard eyes upon him. "Is this the guy Alexa told me about?"

Rand uncoiled his tall frame, placing a seemingly friendly hand on Troy's arm as he stood. The touch didn't fool him for a second. It was a warning to Troy to relax and a message to the other two that, for the moment at least, Troy was under his protection. "Yeah, this is Troy Lansing, a visitor from another pack in the state. Troy, this is Jesse Farrell and Charlie Aquino. They work at the local sheriff's office and are mated members of the pack."

Troy couldn't mask his surprise. Moonlight permitted humans to join their pack? His father had even less time for humans than he did for submissives. If a member of the Brighton pack showed interest in a human, they were threatened, ostracized, and often killed. The humans never survived. Clark believed wholeheartedly in the superiority of shifters as a race, and nothing could be allowed to water down their bloodlines. Troy thought he was a bigoted fool, but he'd made sure to steer clear of human females. He had enough blood on his hands.

The cops gave him a thorough looking over. Neither offered their hand to shake. The blond, Jesse, turned to Rand. "Alexa should have that research you wanted ready by this evening. Why don't you swing by and we can have dinner together? She and Hannah can run through everything they've gathered, and we can discuss this new case at the same time."

"Sounds good." Rand squeezed Troy's shoulder, steering him down the steps and past the two men. "We're heading over to see Knox for a bit. I'll catch you later." He pointed Troy in the direction of the garage on the opposite side of the road, raising the hand clutching his cup to acknowledge the good-byes of the humans.

"You don't have a lot of humans in your pack, I take it?" Rand asked. The up-and-over shutter of the garage stood open, but they stopped outside the workshop area.

"Try none. My father is something of a

traditionalist," Troy muttered, peering into the shadowy interior. Bits and pieces of a car lay strewn across the concrete floor. He admired the crisp cream leather of a pair of seats, very similar to the ones he'd had custom-made for his car...son of a bitch! The metal jigsaw scattered in front of him was the remains of his pride and joy. His baby.

"Hey, Rand." The big guy who'd taken possession of his car keys loomed out of the shadows. His buzz-cut and frown gave him a menacing air, and Troy shifted his balance. Rolling onto the balls of his feet in a preparatory move, just in case. "Relax, man," Knox drawled. "I'm pretty sure I can put everything back in the right place." He wiped his hands on a greasy rag in his back pocket then propped them on his hips. The pose sent his biceps bulging, threatening to rip the seams of the dark T-shirt he wore.

Staring past Troy, he spoke to Rand. "I didn't find anything other than a memory stick holding a dubious choice in driving tunes."

Troy bristled. There was nothing wrong with Enya. A man needed something to relax him when he covered the amount of miles he did. Casting a look toward Knox, he waited for the mechanic to give him a nod before he entered the relative cool of the workshop. Crouching down, he checked the bodywork sections nearest to him. They were pristine, not a mark on them, and he sighed in relief. It might be a one-horse town, but Knox knew his way around cars and had treated the vehicle with respect.

Making a show of inspecting the various chunks of his car, he turned his thoughts inward. The mechanic needed adding to his list of potential threats. The pair of cops, too. Moonlight had more than its fair share of large, dominant males for such a small pack. Glancing over his shoulder, he watched the easy way the two wolves interacted with each other. They had the same sense of connection he'd noticed everywhere today. Another weapon in their favor. Such closeness would help them work as a pack, a cohesive unit. Clark encouraged Brighton pack members to spy on each other, to report any hint of betrayal or disloyalty. Neighbors closed their doors to one another, friendships were sacrificed in the name of survival. You only had to look at his own family. The four children of the alpha stuck to their own assigned roles and presented a careful façade to each other. Without the bond he shared with his younger sister, there would be no one to mourn him if he fell. No one who would step in to defend him unless they saw an advantage to themselves. Intrigue and betrayal versus loyalty and unity. If he couldn't persuade his father to ignore Moonlight, maybe he could play down the threat enough that only a small force was sent against them. It would give Derek and the others a chance to survive, a chance to escape before the main force of the Brighton pack swept down upon them. It might be their only hope.

Chapter Six

Forty-eight hours. She'd managed to stay away from Troy for the sum total of two days, and here she was begging for scraps at his door. Shaking her head in disgust at herself, Bel turned away, intent on returning to the sanctuary of her bungalow. Yesterday had passed in a fitful blur, the aftermath of her flame out. Derek had stopped by long enough to check she was okay but hadn't talked about anything other than her direct health. Having been assured she was fine, he'd left her alone.

"Good evening, *ma belle*." The husky sound of Troy's voice sent a shiver down her spine.

Damn it.

Unable to find any sensible recourse, she turned to face him. "Good evening, Troy. I made too much supper and thought you might like some." She thrust the casserole dish in her hands at him, trying not to squirm at the untruth. The food had been dropped off earlier by Silver, Kirk's mate. The sweet human had assuaged any lingering fear she might have had about how her projecting had affected the rest of the pack. Giggling over the look of shock on Kirk's face when she'd swung for him, Silver also admitted to pouncing on him the moment he'd returned. The woman had shared way more information than Bel had needed to know, although the idea of being tied to a set of wall bars intrigued her. Kirk's makeshift gym set up in their cabin afforded itself to a range of kinky activities, according to Silver.

Bel could still feel the damp cotton of her dress binding her hands together, restraining her in a way she'd never experienced before. A hot flush rose on her cheeks, and she lifted her hands to try and cover her face, only to realize she still clutched the casserole dish.

"I've already eaten, thank you." Troy lounged against the doorframe, hands thrust into the pockets of his cargo shorts. He looked cool and collected, and she felt even more of a fool.

"Oh well, never mind. I can put it in the refrigerator for tomorrow." She stepped back, freezing when his hand shot out to grasp her wrist. He didn't speak, just held her there until she wanted to scream with frustration. Forcing her emotions aside, she concentrated on him, using the point where he held her as a focus. Anger, desire, frustration. He mirrored her own feelings so closely she wondered if she was projecting again. "Tell me what you want," she whispered, closing her eyes briefly against the burn of unshed tears.

"It's not about what I want, *ma belle*. It's about what I can have." His thumb slid along the underside of her wrist, massaging her pulse point in slow circles.

You can have me. She held the words in tight, fear of rejection keeping her mute. Fear of something more, too. She hadn't been able to think about anything other than him all day. From the moment she awoke in a tangle of sweaty sheets, heart pounding at the erotic dreams her mind had spun, he'd filled her head. One by one, she'd watched her pack mates find their other halves, teased them even over their instant connection with their mates. Hadn't expected it for herself, hadn't looked for it at all. Content to serve and soothe her pack, she didn't want to give up her place among them. And that's what mating with this man would mean, even if he wanted the same thing and felt the same electric attraction she did. Troy was the son of an alpha, an heir to his pack, and his place would naturally be at his father's side. How could she expect him to give it all up to settle in a backwater town like Moonlight? So why was she here? Why was she risking everything she held dear to be with a man she didn't know, worse still, didn't trust? He was an enigma. A man at war with himself.

"Let me go, Troy." Tugging against his hold, she didn't care when the dish tipped in her hands, sending gravy slopping over the edge onto her fingers.

"I can't." He sighed, a sound full of regret, full of longing.

"Then take me." She forced herself to meet his eyes, staring deep into the warm, green depths. Pushing her fears aside, she drew on the quiet strength of her wolf, called it forth until she knew he would see the other half peeking out. *Take me, take us. We are mates. Look in your heart and you will see it, too.*

He made a rough sound deep in his throat,

turning her body to liquid in an instant. Snatching the dish from her hands, he yanked her forward so she stumbled across the threshold into the solid heat of his chest. He dumped the casserole on a side table to free his hands. Cupping her face, he dragged her up on tiptoe to meet his mouth.

The moment their lips touched, she realized this was the first time he'd kissed her. His tongue thrust deep and he ravished her mouth, probing and tasting her in a hot brand of ownership. She raised her hands, clinging to his shoulders as her knees buckled in the face of his onslaught. He twisted her head, putting her at the exact angle he wanted, diving into her over and over again. She needed to breathe, the tightness in her chest warned her, but she didn't care. Curling her tongue over, around, under his, she met him thrust for thrust until the edge of her vision started to fade into gray haze. Yanking away at last, he dragged air into his lungs on a deep, whooping gasp. Bel collapsed against him, chest heaving like a bellows. The rampant lust between them had ignited the moment he touched her, spiraling out of her control. Counting under her breath, she fought to slow her racing heart, resisting when he would have pulled her up for another kiss. His arms curled around her back, his touch shifting from demanding to comforting and she scrambled to rein in her emotions.

"This is a mistake," he muttered into her hair. She nodded against his shoulder, knowing he was right. His hands slid lower, tracing the curves of her ass, cupping and kneading the plump flesh.

The hard length of his erection poked her belly, and she pressed into it. "I can't think when I'm around you. My wolf is driving me crazy."

"God, mine, too," he groaned. "I feel unhinged, this isn't me." His hands stilled their incessant stroking. "Did you do something to me?" He stepped back, the distance between them giving her room to breathe. A suspicious frown marred his normally open countenance. "Tell me what it means to be an omega, Bel."

Her wolf rubbed against the inside of her skin, urging her to pounce, to throw herself into her mate's arms and drive the doubts and fears from him. *Make him claim us.* Reaching for the tangle of emotions curled like a fist beneath her breastbone, Bel focused on the burning lust overwhelming her common sense. She batted aside her wolf when it snapped and snarled, dialing back the riot of feelings until she felt calm enough to speak. "Being omega might mean different things to others, I don't know, I've never met another shifter like me. I can sense strong emotions in others. If I focus hard enough, I can also boost or dampen them. So if a member of the pack is grieving or stressed out, I can offer them some respite." She paused. It was always hard to explain something so instinctive. "I don't steal their feelings or make them go away, but I can turn down the volume a bit, if that makes sense."

He scrubbed a hand across his face, massaging the deep frown lines between his brows. She longed to reach out, to help him relax, but she had learned in the past to temper her need to help everyone. She couldn't fix everything, shouldn't *try* to fix everything. Her pack trusted her to guard their secrets and let them make their own choice to seek her out. The only time she acted against a person's will was at the strict instruction of her alpha, and then only if doing so would prevent violence or irreparable harm. An alpha with less nobility though? She shuddered. It didn't bear thinking about.

"So what I feel when I'm around you?"

"I can't manipulate you into feeling an emotion that isn't there." She sighed. He deserved to know the full truth. "But I can amplify your feelings. I'm drawn to you, Troy. More so than to any other man I have met. My wolf...." She shook her head, not ready to acknowledge out loud the possibility they might be mates.

He turned away, paced the length of the open-plan room through the kitchen area, and pulled open the back door. The warm, humid atmosphere in the room lifted, stirred by a faint breeze. Keeping his back to her, he rested his head against the frame, staring out into the dusky half-light. "Are you doing it now, amplifying what I'm feeling?"

Her immediate reaction was to deny it, but she had promised herself she would be honest with him. She checked her mental shields and found them intact. Checked her wolf, who turned away from her, making its feelings plain. "I am not interfering with you in any way."

Growling, he spun around, fists clenched, a vein popping on his forehead. He looked so fierce she took an involuntary step back. "Then why can't I control myself? Why can't I think about anything other than tying you to my bed and fucking you for hours?"

Avoiding his heated stare, she let her eyes trace down his broad chest, and lower. Big mistake. The ridge of his cock pressed against the thin cotton of his shorts. Unable to tear her gaze away, she licked her lips, remembering the sensation of his cock driving into her pussy, filling her to the limit and pushing her to ecstasy. Cracks appeared in her inner shields, and the passion she felt for him came roaring to the forefront.

"Stop looking at me like that, *ma belle*," he begged.

"I can't." She turned his earlier words back upon him. Her pulse fluttered in her throat, an answering throb started between her legs, and she tilted her head to the side, offering him her vulnerable pulse point in an act of surrender and submission. He crossed the room in a single leap, taking her to the floor with him, using his strong arms to protect her back as they hit the terracotta tile. He fixed his open mouth over the place where her neck curved into her shoulder and sucked hard, pressing the edge of his teeth into the skin to breaking point. She arched her back, rubbing her breasts against the hard wall of his chest, curling her ankles around his hips so his lower body rested in the cradle of hers. Licking and sucking, he trailed his lips lower, over her collarbone, pausing at the hollow at the base of her throat, lower still. Encountering the top of her T-shirt, he grabbed the material, rending it in two. The tattered remnants fell away, leaving her bared to the waist for his hungry mouth.

The edge of his claws kissed her skin as he curled his hands around her torso, lifting her body closer to the questing hunger of his mouth. Biting down over her left nipple, he growled, sending vibrations through the sensitive nerve endings. She cried out, burying her hands into the thick waves of his hair, holding him closer. He ground against her hips, driving the breath from her lungs, leaving her panting and sobbing for him to touch her, take her, claim her. There was no turning back now. She would give him everything, to the exclusion of all things, including loyalty to her pack. Her brain tried to seize on that threat, but she pushed it away. No thinking, no doubting, only this. Only heat and wet and pleasure, with an edge of pain. He could consume her, use her until her body collapsed, and she would thank him for it. Madness. Perfection. Bliss.

Holding her by the waist, he rolled them both, putting his back to the hard floor, leaving her sprawled over the front of his body. She put her hands on his shoulders and used his body as leverage to sit up, rocking her sex against him. The juices from her pussy soaked through her panties and the front of his shorts. He yanked the sides of her skirt up, reached beneath to find the thin cotton of her panties, and dragged the material free of her body. Rising on her knees, she fumbled at the waistband of his shorts, sending the button flying in her haste to undo it. In a clash of hands and panting laughter, they both tugged and shoved at his shorts until they slid over his hips, freeing his cock into her eager grasp. The heat of it scorched the center of her palms, and she let loose a greedy moan at her first sight of him in the light cast by the lamp on a nearby table.

She encircled him with both hands, covering his cock from root to tip, teasing the head with the side of her thumb. He lifted his hips, pushing into her touch, and a drop of liquid glistened at in the slit. Capturing it with her thumb, she raised it to her mouth, staring deep into his eyes as she tasted the savory essence of him.

"Fucking witch." He gasped, and she laughed in delight. This man, this glorious, masculine other half of her soul was as bewitched as she was. She stroked his flesh in slow, twisting drags of one hand, easing the other between their bodies to cup his heavy balls.

"Get up here," he ordered. "I can smell your sweet pussy, feel you creaming all over my thigh, and it's making me crazy." He licked his lips, drew the lower one between his teeth, and her clit throbbed in response.

She pushed to her feet, unbuttoned and shed her skirt as quickly as possible, shrugging the remains of her top from her shoulders. Taking her cue, he was naked in moments, tossing his discarded clothing on the floor. Settling onto his back, he beckoned her to him with one finger. Turning to face his feet, she sank to her knees, straddling his upper chest so her mouth was in line with the heated flesh of his cock.

His hot breath ghosted between her spread thighs. She bent her head, sucking him into her mouth at the same moment he slid his tongue the entire length of her sex. She moaned, taking him deeper until she nearly choked. Easing back, she grasped his cock at the base, squeezing gently while she traced the underside of the broad head. She found the little notch, pressed the tip of her tongue deeper into it, dragging a growl from his throat. Strong hands gripped her ass, holding her in place, and he speared his tongue into the depths of her core, fucking in and out of her body in bold, hard strokes. Pushing her hips back, she rode his hot mouth, tilting her body farther forward to swallow the silken length of his cock. She slid her mouth down to where her hand gripped him, and swallowed again. Relaxing her mouth, she played her tongue up and down, licking and lapping at the gorgeous treat. Musk and clean sweat filled her lungs, combining with the fresh tang of his natural eucalyptus scent to drive her higher.

She rocked backward and forward, into his mouth, back down onto his cock, chasing her pleasure, but it remained tantalizingly out of reach. She needed more. The passion in her heart built, swelled, overtopped her like a cresting wave and rose higher still. She felt mad with it, burned with it, and still she could not find her peak. Lifting her head, she gasped for breath. "Troy, help me."

Chapter Seven

The desperate pleading in Bel's tone shook Troy from his sexual frenzy. The taste of her, the feel of her hot, sweet mouth enveloping his cock, the savage urging of his wolf had combined again to drive all thought from his brain. Dropping his head back on the floor, he panted hard, trying to gather his scattered wits. *Take her, claim her.* His wolf snarled and writhed beneath his skin, giving him a slash with its mental claws when he shoved the creature's lustful demands back. Shifting his hands from her ass to her waist, he lifted Bel away from the aching throb of his cock. He sat up, pulling her into his lap. Wrapping his arms around her waist, he held her back to his chest, pressing soothing kisses to her shoulder until she quietened. A couple more shuddering breaths rattled through her, but, eventually, she relaxed into his hold and leaned against his shoulder.

"All right, *ma belle*?" He nuzzled beneath her ear, and she sighed softly.

"I didn't mean to lose control," she whispered. "I thought I had it locked down, but from the moment you touched me, I felt like I was burning up."

He cuddled her close. He knew what she meant. His whole life had been a hard lesson in suppressing his emotions and keeping a tight rein upon himself and his wolf. This tiny woman unmanned him, made him break all his self-imposed rules. Nothing and no one mattered when the sweet tang of her arousal filled his senses. "I want to say to you there will be another chance for us. A better time when we can relax and put pack and duty aside to focus on this thing between us." He ran his hands up and down her arms, soothing her, soothing himself with the rhythmic action.

"You'd be lying though," she murmured, turning her head to press a kiss to the underside of his chin.

"I can't let you go, Bel. I know I should, but I can't. I won't." He twisted her in his lap to stare into the vivid blue of her eyes. "It's too soon to say this, ridiculous to even entertain the thought, but my wolf is screaming at me." He lifted his hand, brushing the tangled bangs of her blonde hair back from her forehead. Cupping the back of her head, he drew her forward until they rested brow to brow.

"Mates." Her quiet voice rang with sincerity, and the tight grip of panic in his chest eased. She felt it, too.

An unlucky stroke of fate had brought them together, but he could not find it in himself to curse it. The gift of a mate should never be taken for granted. Acknowledging the truth of their situation crystalized the rest of his path. He could not take her home to Brighton. He would not give his father the chance to corrupt her. And he would. Once he understood the power and advantage someone with her gifts could give him, there would be no stopping Clark Lansing. He'd force Bel to manipulate others, use her up and spit out whatever broken dregs of her soul remained.

He had to find a way to escape. Hoped Derek would take him and Quinn into his pack. His father wouldn't give them up without a fight, nor would he give up on his plans to conquer the Moonlight pack and bring them under his control. Those worries could wait, though. For tonight, his mate needed reassurance, and he needed to claim her. Tucking his arms beneath her knees, Troy shifted his weight and pushed to his feet, lifting Bel with him. Her arms curled around his neck, and he carried her through the small cottage to his bedroom.

Night had fallen, and a gentle breeze stirred the thin drapes he'd drawn over the open windows. They'd kept the worst of the sun's heat out, leaving the room marginally cooler than the rest of the house. He lowered Bel to the center of his bed then moved around the room, opening the curtains to let the soft light of the rising moon illuminate the bed. Its silvery rays danced across her skin, creating a map of shadows and plains his mouth watered to explore. No longer fettered, his wolf settled calmly upon him, gifting him with its enhanced senses. Being in harmony with his other half again loosened another tight fist of tension within him. Walking to the end of the bed, he pressed his knees against the soft edge of the mattress, but refrained from climbing onto it. "Show me what you've got, *ma belle*," he urged.

She pressed her lips together for a moment. Her gaze danced away, back again to meet his, and he let himself go. He was asking his mate to be vulnerable before him; the least he could do was offer the same in return. Shedding the easy charm, the laughing mask he wore to protect himself, he showed her everything. Showed her the scared, scarred man who longed only for a moment of peace.

"Oh, Troy." The soft rays of the moon glinted on the tears gathering in her eyes.

He wanted to turn away, wanted to hide his face and shield his vulnerable heart, but she deserved his truth. Holding her eyes, he opened his palms, extending them at his sides. *Here I am. Will you take me? Will you take this damaged soul and make me whole again?*

She held out her hand to him, spreading her thighs as she did so, offering her body, and he hoped, her heart, accepting his in return. He crawled onto the bed, settled between her legs, and braced his weight over her. Pressing her thumbs to the corner of his eyes, she wiped away tears he hadn't known were forming and tugged his face down to meet hers. Their lips brushed together, once, twice, a soft affirmation. He kissed her slowly, softly, putting all the hopes and fears in his heart into that soft melding of lips and tongues. Drawing her lower lip between his own, he sucked, pressing his lower body down to meet her rising hips. He ran his tongue behind her lip, tracing each undulation of her sensitive gums, asking for more, claiming every tiny surrender she gave him. Sweeping deep, he curled his tongue around hers, tugging it back into his own mouth. This was to be a partnership of equals; he would surrender all to her in return.

They kissed and petted for what seemed like hours, and he was content. Wolves needed play as much as they needed sex, and they rolled together on the sheets like teenagers too nervous to take the next step. She tangled their legs together, trying to use her slight weight to flip over and pin him on his back, and he acquiesced. His willingness to submit was justly rewarded when she slithered down the front of his body and drew his cock into the tender heat of her mouth. Folding his arms behind his neck to resist the urge to grab her head and drive into the silken depths, he stared down his body at her. The feather-soft curls of her blonde hair tickled against his groin, adding another layer of sensation to the sweet, eager lap of her tongue, the heated suction of her mouth. Using the tips of her nails, she scored the solid muscles of his thighs, digging and pressing into the hard flesh as she feasted upon him.

The sight of her wet lips sliding up and down his shaft drew his balls up tight, and he knew he wouldn't last much longer. She glanced up at him, the wicked glint in her eyes telling him she knew exactly how close he was to coming. Increasing the pressure, she dragged her mouth upward until she held just the thick head of his cock between her lips. She circled her tongue, lapping and probing across the tortured nerve endings before releasing him with a loud pop.

"Get up here," he growled, desperate to touch and taste and take her.

Shaking her hair away from her face, she laughed, a golden sound of triumph and pleasure and he was lost to her. She perched across his legs, stroking the sensitive skin around the top of his thighs, chasing a ripple of tension through his lower abdomen with her dancing fingertips. His cock pulsed and twitched, like a dog blindly following its master, begging for attention. He curled his fingers through the wooden slats of the headboard, bracing against his dominant need to flip her over and rut his way to completion in the molten depths of her pussy. This was Bel's show and he would let her have her head. If only she would give him more.

Bracing herself with one hand on his thigh, she lifted her spread hips, giving him a glimpse of her sex, glistening wet and plumped with blood. Pushing one finger into her mouth, she licked and sucked it, pouting her lips until they shone like her pussy. She traced the damp digit over her lower lip, down her chin, throat, and torso in a wanton display. He growled his encouragement. Damn, she was the sexiest fucking thing he had ever seen and he loved watching her own her sexuality, claiming her right to pleasure and enjoyment. Her finger circled her clit. Lifting her hips again, she made sure he had a good view as her hand slid lower and her fingers disappeared into her core. Her head rolled back, baring her creamy throat and she moaned aloud, shuttling her fingers faster, deeper, fucking herself.

A sharp snap sounded by his ear, and he threw away the broken slat of the headboard. With his hand free now, he couldn't persuade himself to keep still any longer and he sat up, grasping her around the waist to both support her and arch her back so he could suck her breast into his mouth. He tongued her nipple, teasing the bundle of nerves over and over, palming her other breast to massage the tender flesh. She pulled her fingers from her pussy, and pressed her upper body forward to sit up until he had no choice but to release her nipple. Eyes shining with excitement and anticipation, she painted the delicious, spicy taste of her sex over his mouth and he sucked her fingers between his lips, licking up every drop of her cream.

Tugging her forward, he settled her hips over his, let her find her balance again on her knees, then thrust up through the hot, plump tissues of her sex and into heaven. Eyes locked, they rocked together in slow, conscious movements. He needed to pause, to savor the silken stretch of her body as it welcomed him in. She shifted from hip to hip, adjusting her legs until she sat fully in his lap, legs curled around him, heels seated against his ass. Her hands slid up his spine, touching each knot of bone, testing the thick slabs of muscles on either side until her arms curved up and under his arms, hands locked over his shoulders for leverage. The sharp pinch of her nails as she dug them in, lifting and lowering herself on his cock, sent a hot rush of animal pleasure through him. His mate would leave her mark on him, something to show other females he was taken, claimed, and it spoke to the most fundamental part of his being. Nudging her hair to the side, he burrowed his face into the base of her neck, seeking the perfect spot. He closed his mouth around her pulse point, biting down into her soft skin, relishing the iron tang of her blood. She threw her head back, screaming his name as she drove down to meet his upward thrust, the hot muscles of her sex squeezing his cock in a velvet fist of demand.

He thrust again and again, holding her hips tight so he could press deeper, setting off another rippling wave that dragged him under with her this time. His seed poured forth, marking her with his scent as he marked her with his teeth. *Mine. Mine. Always mine.*

The words echoed in his head, punctuating every jerk of his hips. His wolf snarled, pushing beneath his skin. The beast within wanted to shift, wanted to chase their mate through the woods, take her and claim her animal to animal and complete the final step toward full mating. *Soon*, he promised. Forcing his locked jaw to relax, Troy used his tongue to gently soothe the deep bite on Bel's shoulder, encouraging her rapid healing abilities to start. He'd pressed his teeth in hard enough to scar and though the mark would fade, she would carry it always. His claim.

She nuzzled against him, licking the sweat from his chest, tracing a path to his throat. He turned his head, offering himself to her. He'd sworn they would be equals and he meant it. The edge of her teeth scraped his skin, sending his softening cock into painful rigidity inside her. She moaned, a hot mutter of his name against his skin and circled her hips, taking him as deep as he could go. Using just her inner muscles, she worked her pussy over and around him, massaging and squeezing his shaft, licking and teasing along his shoulder joint at the same time.

"You're fucking killing me, *ma belle*," he groaned, and she let loose a throaty chuckle. His mate was the most delicious cock tease to ever grace the planet. He would die a happy man. Lifting her face from his shoulder, she grabbed his chin, holding him still to meet her gaze. Fucking him slowly, she softened her grip, stroked his cheek, his temple, the thick waves of his hair. The tenderness in her touch broke him wide open and he held his breath, knowing she could destroy him with a single word.

Or save him.

"Mine," she crooned, pressing her lips to the

corner of his mouth. "My mate, my heart, my love."
She punctuated each declaration with a soft kiss
traveling down to the intersection of his neck and
shoulder. "Always." She breathed the word against
his skin, biting deep. Holding his flesh in her mouth,
in her sex, she drew his essence. Blood and seed—life.
He roared her name, pumping his hips, filling her
again and again.

He came to with the pleasant weight of his mate
draped across his body. Holding her close, he buried
his nose in her hair, drawing her sweet scent deep
into his lungs. Their mingled scents filled the room,
blanketed over them in the humid night air. The
sheets beneath him were rumpled, damp with sweat
and other things. He wanted to nail them to his wall
like a damn trophy. As the euphoria faded, the dark
realities pressed against the edges of his conscience.
He had to come clean to Bel. About everything. He
should have done it before, damn him, but he had
been too selfish, too weak to resist the lure of her
sweet body. Stroking his hands up and down her back
he closed his eyes and forced himself to go back to
the source of too many nightmares.

"They came in the middle of the night. Daddy
had been working since the previous morning helping
a newly mated couple to raise the frame on a new
home. Every dominant in our small pack had helped
so they were all exhausted. It was the night before
Quinn's fifth birthday and she couldn't get to sleep.
Momma had planned a big party, and Quinn crawled
in to bed with me to whisper about everything." He
paused, lost for a moment in the memory of his little
sister huddled against his side, enjoying those last
moments of innocent peace. "We never knew

anything about the world beyond the boundaries of our pack lands around Sebastian."

Bel raised her head, folded her arms across his chest, and rested her chin on them. Her blue eyes studied him. "I thought your pack was based in the Brighton Reservation?"

He glanced up at the ceiling, unable to watch her reaction to his next words. "After that night, it was. Clark Lansing swept into Sebastian with a pack of his strongest dominants. They set fire to the newly erected frame, causing chaos, drawing parents away from their families. My father knew something was wrong. Told me to take Quinn and hide." He swallowed hard. "I made a mistake. Ran in the wrong direction and they caught us." The malicious gleam in Clark's eyes would be forever seared in his memory. "He knew who we were. It was only growing up that I came to understand how he worked. Every move made against a pack was meticulously planned and researched. Including ours. I made it easy for him."

Bel gave a soft sound of protest, but he knew the truth of it.

He shrugged off her sympathetic hand and forced himself to continue. "They'd already killed the alpha. Wiped out his entire family before they set the fire. Dad was second. A strong beta wolf, but with too much heart to be alpha." His love for his family had undone them all. "Clark threatened to kill us unless my father surrendered the pack to him. Momma went crazy. She shifted and attacked the man holding Quinn, and they shot her." The bark of the gun, the stink of powder and blood, his sister's screams. Memory after memory washed over him, dragging him under, bringing the terrified boy of his past to the forefront. The wolf holding Quinn had died before they put one too many bullets in his father. He could see him clearly, hear his voice whispering in his ear as the last breath left him. *"You do whatever it takes to survive, son."*

Wetness rolled down his cheeks, soaking into the pillow behind his head, the way his father's blood had soaked into the dust that night. Warmth stole over him, a blanket of comfort settling around him, muffling the grief. He blinked away the tears, looked down at the spot over his heart where Bel pressed her small hand into his skin. The warmth came from her, and he understood the beauty of her omega gift. Rolling on his side, he spooned around her body, grounding himself in the feel of his mate in his arms.

Whatever it takes.

Chapter Eight

Bel darted through the trees, grateful for their shade as she tried to run off the worst of the tension squeezing around her heart. Troy had fallen into a deep sleep after his whispered confession, holding her tight enough for it to be uncomfortable. She hadn't protested, though. If her mate needed something to cling onto to drive the bad memories away, she would endure without complaint. The pain he'd suffered as a child, combined with the survivor's guilt of his adulthood, had left a deep bruise on his soul. She'd sensed it the moment she'd reached out to ease his distress, had almost buckled under the devastation of it.

A familiar scent touched her nose, and she raised her muzzle to track the owner. A large, black wolf stepped between two huge oaks, holding his ground until she turned and trotted in his direction. Bel raised her head offering her throat, showing respect and deference to her alpha. Derek pressed his snout into the thick fur at her neck for a moment then withdrew. His golden eyes stared hard at her, his scent a mix of anger and concern.

Where is Troy? Wolves could speak mind to mind, and she couldn't help herself. He'd slipped from his bed early that morning, determined to present himself to Derek and explain everything. He'd refused to let her go with him. He would not let any affection the alpha held for Bel temper his response to what Troy had to say to him. She appreciated him not putting her in the position of being caught between mate and alpha, but the morning had passed in slow, creeping increments until she'd had to shift and go for a run.

He is with Rand. Troy is making a call to his father, after which we will hold another meeting to discuss what happens next.

The alpha wolf stepped forward, crowding into her space. *I cannot give my support to this mating, Bel.*

Do not force me to choose, Derek. It would break my heart to leave Moonlight, to leave our pack that I love so dearly.

The black wolf snarled, a deep warning rumble. *You are still my wolf, Bel. I will not let you go without a fight.*

Her heart sank. It appeared the alpha had rejected Troy's plea for sanctuary for himself and Quinn within the Moonlight pack. *Then don't fight. Is there no way we can work together to defeat the threat from Brighton?* Even as she sent the thought, her heart twisted at the selfishness of her request. They had faced so many threats in the past, had fled to Florida to escape the predations of another cruel and power-hungry alpha. She couldn't ask Derek to put the pack at risk again. *I'm sorry. Just let us go and Troy and I will run far from here. We'll leave the area, the state if we have to.*

It's too late for that.

Realization struck, making her stagger as though from a physical blow. It didn't matter whether Troy and she left, Clark would not give up his designs on conquering her friends and family. A soft whine escaped her throat and Derek closed in, resting his proud head over her back, tucking her close against his strong, reassuring body.

Hush now, Bel. Let us see what Lansing has to say in response to Troy's suggestion of an accord between our packs. I will not bow my head to him, nor allow him to assume alpha status over any of my wolves, but I will work with the devil himself if it keeps my pack safe.

Bel leaned closer into Derek's side. She had been sheltered her whole life under his protection, and he gave her the support she needed again. Regardless of the imminent threat to their safety, he didn't rush her, standing still and sure while she gathered herself together. A slight shift in her weight was all the signal he needed to lift his head.

Trust me, Bel, and I will trust you. I cannot believe your mate would betray us, so together we must find a way to keep everyone safe.

Wishing she could find an ounce of the confidence her alpha had, she nodded her head. Derek gripped her muzzle gently between his jaws then released her, turning to lope through the trees. He didn't head back to town but farther into the woods.

Catching the scent of a rabbit, Bel yipped and darted forward, following the trail. First, they would hunt as wolves, then they would test their human wits and hope they could come out on top and not end up prey themselves.

***

The brightly patterned headscarf protected her hair from the worst ravages of the wind whipping through the convertible. She glanced sideways at Troy, seeking reassurance. Every mile of asphalt that passed beneath the wheels increased the butterflies in her stomach. Keeping his eyes fixed on the highway, Troy reached for her hand, kissed the back of it, and placed it on his thigh. The heat of his skin soaked through the linen pants he wore, and the familiar feel of the sculpted muscle beneath her fingers helped to ground her. The trip to Brighton would only take a couple of hours. They should be back safe in Moonlight before nightfall.

Clark's insistence on meeting her had thrown her pack into uproar. Troy had done his best to deflect him, but a request to meet his future daughter-in-law before any official mating ceremony took place was, on the surface, perfectly reasonable. To refuse to go would make him suspicious, and, given some of the stories Troy had shared with her, paranoia was a default state of mind for the Brighton alpha. Mating ceremonies had fallen out of fashion over the years, but they hoped to convince Clark their desire to hold one was an act of deference to his position and a demonstration from Moonlight that they wished to cooperate with their larger neighbor. Their entire plan hinged on the next few hours, and Bel knew she needed to be on top of everything if they were going to be successful. There were so many bluffs and double-bluffs in play, it would be easy to trip up on one of their many lies. Wolves were good at sniffing out duplicity, and, although Troy possessed admirable diplomatic skills, Derek was worried he was too emotionally invested to properly school himself. After some experimentation, Bel believed they'd found a work-around, but time would tell.

Signs of civilization thinned once they turned onto the county road, and the landscape grew wilder on either side of the two-lane road. "We'll be another quarter hour or so. Do you need to stop before we get there?"

She appreciated his concern, but Bel had put together a meditation specifically for today. It had taken Knox a couple of days to put Troy's car back together, complete with a tracker. Her hand drifted to the blue sandstone pendant nestled at the base of her throat. Troy had a pair of matching cufflinks securing the wrists of his crisp, white shirt. Mating gifts from Derek that just happened to contain personal tracking devices. Her pack mates were well versed in surveillance and security techniques. Derek and Rand ran a successful security agency, The Defenders, and Rand in particular was always keen to play with new toys and gadgets. Bel took a deep breath and closed her eyes, turning her focus inward. Knowing her pack monitored their every step gave her the comfort she needed to push her fears aside.

Turning first to her wolf, she communed with the wild spirit of her other half. She needed complete control over every aspect of herself if their plan was to succeed. Her wolf had always been placid, content to serve the dominants, knowing they respected and valued her for having a different type of strength to theirs. Troy had stirred something deeper, something neither wolf nor woman had suspected lurked within them. A fortitude to rival any dominant. The threat of an alpha like Clark abusing their gift had never occurred to them. Even when the pack had faced other enemies, none possessed the twisted scope of the Brighton alpha. Bel had never considered herself a weapon before, but she did now. She could control it, forge and wield her ability to her own design. Or surrender and be both abused and abuser. *Never,* growled her wolf, and Bel curled her lip in agreement.

Reaching out, she brushed her awareness against Troy's, a gentle breath, nothing more. She waited. A silken touch stirred the deep well of desire she held for him, and her eyes flew open as she gasped for breath. Need rippled across the surface, sending her nipples into stiff peaks beneath the white Broderie Anglaise dress she had paired with navy wedge sandals. The high neckline and long sleeves conveyed a modesty she didn't feel around her mate. It looked fresh, respectable without being prissy, and she felt comfortable and relaxed in it. Her outfit contrasted and complemented the dark linen suit Troy wore, and the white cotton glowed against her tanned skin. She'd lacquered her nails with a sheer polish containing tiny holographic bits of glitter which sparkled in the light. A bit of glitz, her personal armor.

She dug her fingers into Troy's thigh, giving him the edge of her nails, knowing it would drive him a little crazy. Turnabout was fair play, and she giggled when a low growl rumbled in his chest.

"Behave, *ma belle*. It would be most inappropriate to show up to my father's dinner table reeking of sex and sweat." The promise in his tone melted her further, and she pressed her thighs together to stop the tingle of awareness. "Fuck," he groaned. Leather squeaked in protest, and his knuckles turned white where he gripped the steering wheel. "Save it for the journey home, baby."

She closed her eyes and used her ability to smother the lust threatening to overwhelm them both. Adding subtle layers, she constructed a mental bridge between them. Building a connection she could use to control their outwardly projected emotions was one of the things they experimented with over the past couple of days. They could lie with impunity and not even Derek had been able to sense it. They had no guarantee it would hold together in a stressful environment, but she would give it her best shot. The surface beneath the wheels changed again, causing the car to bounce around. Concentration broken, she opened her eyes. Thick trees lined the narrow single-track lane, blocking her view of her surroundings. The avenue of trees hung low and stretched long enough to give her the first faint stirrings of claustrophobia. Anything could be within feet of their vehicle and they'd never know it. Just as her heart began to flutter, the vista expanded before her and her mouth dropped open in shock.

A huge buttermilk-colored mansion sprawled at the end of a sweeping circular driveway. An ostentatious fountain, covered in every manner of mythological sea beast, spewed water in the center of the drive. Pillars, turrets, and balconies littered the front of the mansion in a spectacular collision of architectural styles. Gaudy was the politest word she could think of to describe it. The amount of money to construct and maintain such a building boggled her mind.

"You didn't tell me your pack lived together," she murmured as Troy parked at the bottom of an imposing sweep of stairs leading to the front door. Some packs stuck to the old ways and lived in large or interconnected dwellings, mimicking the dens of their shifter natures. Others, like Moonlight, chose to live co-located, finding an acceptable compromise between security and personal privacy.

Troy pressed a button to activate the automatic roof on the convertible and shoved open his door. "They don't. This is my father's house, not a pack house," he said over his shoulder as he climbed out. Rounding the hood toward her side of the car, he tossed his keys to a young man who came scurrying around the side of the house.

What a terrible waste of money. Fixing a smile on her face, Bel accepted the hand Troy held out to her and stepped out of the car. He leaned across to brush his lips over her cheek.

"You look like a fifties movie star," he murmured.

She lifted her hand to his cheek, holding his face against hers for a moment.

"There you are." An imposing voice laced with an alpha's command pulled her entire attention away from her mate. Clark Lansing stood at the top of the stairs. He looked outwardly relaxed with his hands tucked into the side pockets of his sharply tailored black pants. The collar of his dove-gray silk shirt lay open, displaying a red cravat folded and pinned with a huge diamond. His gray hair was brushed back away from his face in two sweeping wings. Nothing friendly shone in his black eyes.

"Father." Troy placed his hand at the base of Bel's back, and she allowed him to propel her up the steps. "This is Belinda Thomas."

Refusing to acknowledge the sour smell emanating from the alpha, Bel turned up her smile a notch and offered her hand. "It is a pleasure to meet you, Mr. Lansing." Simple statements from each of them, as agreed. Nothing inflammatory, nothing that could be interpreted by Clark as either challenge or insult. His hot palm engulfed hers. She had never known her skills to register on an empathetic scale, but malevolence and madness coated her skin like a greasy film. Her wolf shuddered once then pressed forward, comforting Bel as the alpha held her hand and her gaze for an interminable stretch.

"Come now, Father, don't monopolize my soon-to-be sister." A warm, throaty voice shattered the tension.

Bel gritted her teeth at the too-hard squeeze Clark pressed around her fingers before he finally deigned to release her. A cloud of soft-brown hair, warmth, and the pleasing scent of apple blossom enveloped her. It was no effort to return the affectionate embrace from Quinn.

Stepping back, Bel smiled into the woman's green eyes, an almost perfect match to Troy's. "I am so very pleased to meet you. Troy has told me all about you."

"Oh, really?" Quinn threw her head back and laughed, the bright sound lifting Bel's spirits further.

Damn, she's good.

"Nothing too awful, I hope?"

Bel laughed at the teasing question. "He was

perfectly lovely about you," she said, sending Quinn off into another round of laughter. She hooked her arm around Bel's shoulder, guiding her artfully between the two men and into the house. Another man stood sentinel inside the opulent marbled entrance. Bel blinked, taken aback at the sheer size of him. He could challenge her pack-mate Kirk in both height and breadth, something she'd never thought to see.

"This is Nikolas." Quinn waved a too casual hand in his direction, her dismissal of him completely at odds with the tangle of emotions spilling from her.

Glancing at her him over her shoulder, Bel noted Nikolas had eyes for no one but the curvy brunette next to her. *Interesting*.

"Come upstairs to the sitting room, I've ordered some lemonade. You must be parched after your journey."

Bel reached for Troy, not sure whether she should allow Quinn to separate them. His warm voice echoed in her head. *Go, Bel. It's best if I talk to my father alone first.*

He scares me. She couldn't stop the admission.

He scares me too, baby. It's better to let him have his say in private. At least you and Quinn will be out of harm's way.

Quinn's fingers pressed into Bel's shoulder, and she looped her arm around the other woman's waist. They would need to be strong to get through the next few hours. It would help Troy.

I love you. Words she should have said in the quiet dark of their bed, but he needed them now.

You honor me, ma belle.

Chapter Nine

Troy waited at the foot of the stairs. Quinn had shown Bel to the guest bathroom, and he chafed against the delay, needing to get the hell out of there. He hadn't properly acknowledged Bel's stunning declaration of love, fearing his father would see his vulnerability and turn it against him. There would be time enough once he got her safely away. Dinner had been a freak show of forced manners and superficial conversation. Nikolas had contributed little. Never a big talker at the best of times, the rain of blows Clark had landed on his face would be enough to keep anyone quiet. Troy had seen him test his jaw enough to know at least it wasn't broken, but Nik would have a miserable couple of days even with their accelerated healing. His own injuries were mostly confined to his back. Sitting in the car for the next couple of hours was going to suck, but they were leaving the second Bel returned.

"He's asleep." Dutton's soft voice startled him. Foolish to let his guard down for a second in this house of horrors.

"What do you want, Dut?" Troy growled, too

tired and hurt to play any more games.

"He's getting worse." A lock of blond hair tumbled across his brother's forehead, an unforgivable sign of strain. Dutton controlled himself and his wolf more tightly than any other shifter he'd met. On cue, the stray piece of hair was brushed away, set back into place. "Telling him about Belinda's omega nature might have been a mistake. He didn't stop babbling about it until he fell asleep."

The clack of heels on marble warned them of the women's approach. Dutton grabbed Troy's arm, a startling action from a man who schooled his body language. "You cannot bring her home, Troy. If he gets his hands on her, he will destroy her. Destroy us all in the process." His eldest brother slipped into the shadows a second before Quinn and Bel appeared at the top of the stairs. They walked down to him, arms linked in open affection.

After a brief, but fierce hug, Bel stepped back and he could see a hint of moisture in her eyes. She gave a watery laugh. "I'll leave you two to say your good-byes. I'll be outside by the car."

He smiled, grateful at her discretion, watching her until she disappeared from his view.

"She's lovely," Quinn murmured.

Turning with a nod, he gathered his sister close. "She's everything."

He switched to mental communication. *I'm getting us out of here, sis. I can't go into detail yet, but you need to be prepared. After the mating ceremony in Moonlight next week, we won't be coming back here.* He placed her away from him to stare into her eyes. *You, too. Their alpha has agreed to take you into his pack.*

Expecting her to smile, he frowned when she dropped eyes, darting her gaze toward the dining room. The door stood open, the sound of a bottle chinking against a glass carried across the dimly lit hallway. Nikolas had remained at the table when the rest of them had risen, a bottle of scotch in front of him. He'd been with Clark longer than any of them, taken from his pack when still a toddler. He claimed to have no memory of his family and had followed his alpha's every command. Troy didn't want Nik or Dut to suffer their father's predations, but he would not risk his mate or his sister to save them. They would have to find a way to save themselves.

He touched a finger to Quinn's cheek, and she glanced back at him. "Be ready," he whispered, and this time she nodded.

Pressing a kiss to her forehead, he held her close for a few moments more. His wolf wanted him to drag her to the car, get her the hell out of there, but it also understood the need for patience and cunning. Troy had formed a new plan tonight. One he couldn't share with anyone else, not even Bel. Dutton was right; his father could not be allowed to get his hands on her. Nothing else mattered other than keeping her out of his clutches.

They were later than he'd intended. Dusk had fallen and there was little traffic on the rural roads. He listened to Bel make a quick call to Derek. He would know from the trackers they were headed back, but she wanted to make it clear everything was fine. Which was a lie. His back was a blaze of agony from his shoulders to his hips, forcing him to sit upright. He'd lowered the roof again, but this time she hadn't bothered with her scarf. He risked a quick glance across toward her. Tendrils of her hair blew across her face, and she shook her head to release them, offering him a glimpse of her delicate throat. Her face had been turned toward the side window from the moment her seat belt clicked in place, but he didn't need to see the expression on her face. Her low, simmering anger filled the space between them. *Shit.* She'd held the connection between them open throughout his encounter with his father, resisting all his attempts to shut her out of his mind.

"What did he do to you?" She tugged at the restraining hold of the seat belt and twisted around to study him.

He flicked a look at her, wished he hadn't bothered when he saw the pain and torment twisting her features. "I don't want to talk about it."

"Fuck you and what you fucking want. The smell of your blood and pain is sending my wolf crazy. We are going to talk about this, Troy."

The profanity shocked him. His Bel didn't even talk dirty during sex. Humiliation and pent-up fury shot through him and he scanned the side of the road. Spying a dirt road, he yanked the steering wheel, sending the car bouncing down the rutted lane until they couldn't be seen by any passing traffic. He turned off the engine, unclipped his belt, and threw himself out of the car. Bel shot out the vehicle, rounding the hood so they met halfway. Chest to chest, they glared at each other. With a growl of frustration, he dragged the wrinkled linen jacket from his shoulders and tossed it on the ground. If she wanted the truth, he'd damn well show her every ugly fucking stripe of it. Unbuttoning his shirt took too long and he gave up. His fingers were too damn shaky to fiddle with the small pearl discs anyway. He ripped the front open, unable to stifle a cry of pain when the cotton stuck to the dried blood on his back. Shoving away her attempts to stop him, Troy pulled his shirt off and spun around.

"Oh, my love. Oh, what did he do to you?" The shock in her voice stole the anger from him, leaving him naked and vulnerable beneath her gaze. Tears trickled down his face, but he couldn't raise a hand to brush them away, terrified any movement would break the dam he'd built around his heart. Soft fingers and softer kisses traced each livid strap mark across his skin as Bel sought to alleviate the injuries laid down by his father's belt.

Clark had been livid, refusing to listen to anything Troy had to say to him. He was alpha. His children would mate if, when, and to whom he chose. Cursing Troy for his sentimentality, his weakness, his failure to obey orders, Clark had threatened to punish Quinn in his stead. Stripping his clothing and offering his unprotected flesh to the alpha had done the trick.

Nikolas and Dutton had stood by in silence until Troy had fallen to the floor under the force of one too many strikes. Nik had stayed their father's hand at that point, refusing to allow Clark to flay his face. Just as well or Troy would likely have lost an eye, or worse. His intervention had cost him dearly, drawing the last of Clark's seething rage in a flurry of punches. Dutton had pulled out a first-aid kit from a cabinet. Ignoring Clark, while he beat Nikolas bloody, his brother had talked quietly and calmly to Troy as he cleaned the wounds on his back. Through gritted teeth, he'd told Dutton about his observations of the

Moonlight pack. Persuaded him to see the sense in a bloodless coup, rather than a full-out assault.

The mating ceremony would be the perfect cover, they'd reasoned together. Allowing the principals of the Brighton pack to walk right into the center of Moonlight as invited guests. Once Derek was out of the way, the rest of the pack would come to heel, he'd assured them. Lie after lie spilled from his mouth about how weak Moonlight was. How small, how insignificant compared to the strength of Brighton. Every word had fed his father's ego, his madness sated by blood enough for him to join the conversation. Didn't he see how Troy had delivered him the perfect way to assimilate the new pack?

When Clark hesitated, pain and desperation forced Troy to let slip about the gift Bel would bring to their family through her omega abilities. A dark gleam of excitement lit Clark's eyes, and he acquiesced to their plans. Something in his expression had told Troy this was not the first time his father had encountered a wolf like her. He regretted it instantly, but it had been too late to take it back. It was at that moment the new plan coalesced in his mind.

Through it all, Bel held the bridge between them, masking his lies, his fear, his desperation. She'd sat beside him through dinner, making small talk, eating her food, acting for all the world like an excited mate meeting her new family, not realizing he had betrayed her. Forcing himself to move away from her gentle ministrations, Troy hung his head. "He knows about you."

"He had to learn about it sometime." Her simple acceptance floored him. Didn't she understand? Clark had the scent of prey in his nose, and he would hunt Bel to the ends of the earth to possess her. He swung around to face her, to scream his fear and regret of what might now never come to pass between them. The words died in his throat.

She knew.

She stared at him, big blue eyes full of sorrow, but no blame, no censure. Christ, she was incredible, and he didn't deserve her. A wild groan loosed from his throat, and he fell upon her, seeking her mouth, shoving her back against the hood of the car. Like a flower unfurling beneath the sun, she opened her lips, her arms, her heart, and took everything from him. Shoving his tongue deep into the welcoming warmth, he clutched her waist, lifting her up until she perched on the hot metal of the hood. Her thighs fell open, creating a cradle for his thrusting hips. He felt her ankles lock at the base of his spine, heard one of her sandals clatter to the ground behind him as he licked and sucked and probed the wet heat of her mouth. Her fingers dug into the thick muscles of his biceps, pulling him closer until his upper body pinned her against the hard surface of the car.

They rocked together, their grunts and gasps punctuating the still night air. "I need you, Bel," he moaned against her lips, reaching back to unhook her legs.

She raised her hips, giving him room to tug off her panties. He'd barely unfastened the front of his pants before she reached between them to grip the pulsing weight of his cock. He bucked once, sliding between her eager fingers. Feeling the tension melt away at the first kiss of his aching cock against the drenched seam of her sex, he threw back his head and shouted her name, pushing forward into the molten heat of her delicious core. Her hand released him only long enough to clutch his ass, as though she feared he might draw back. He pressed again, sliding deeper, relishing the tight squeeze of her rippling muscles. She deserved better than this, deserved better than a desperate grind against the hood of his car. Jamming her heels against the hot metal, she lifted her hips to him, dropped down, and thrust again. He held still, letting her fuck herself up and down the length of his cock, watching the desire cloud her eyes as her pace increased. Hot little noises burst from her lips. Grunts and sighs and gasps that drove him wild with need for her.

Tucking his hands under her body, he grabbed the plump cheeks of her ass and took over. He ploughed the depths of her pussy, grunting with effort as he drove away the horrors of the day. There was only her, only him, and the slap, slap of flesh on flesh. Her sighing breath, his growling demand for her to come. And she did, milking his cock, dragging his release from the depths of his soul. He shoved his face into her neck, sobbing in relief, and she cuddled him close, rocking them until the storm passed and he could think again.

Lifting his wet face, he stared down at her. "I love you, Belinda."

"I love you, too, Troy. We'll get through this; we'll find a way through. Focus on that, focus on the future we will have together. One more week and this will all be over."

He hid his face in her neck again, afraid she would read the truth in his eyes. A week from now everything would be over, but not in the way she hoped. Her hands cupped his head, pressing him into her throat for one long moment before she dropped them to his shoulders and eased his weight from her body.

"Let's go home." Her lips whispered over his in the softest caress. With a nod he stood up, bent to retrieve her sandals where they'd dropped to the floor, and winced when the movement tugged at the healing skin on his back. "Give me the keys. If you shift, it will accelerate your healing." She finished adjusting the strap on her sandal and glanced up at him through her bangs. "I can drive, you know." She shook her head, muttering about stubborn dominant asshole men as she slid from the hood and straightened her dress.

He hesitated. Everything hurt. His body, his head, his heart. They were still well over an hour from home; he should drive. It was his job to get her safely home.... *God damn it, I am an asshole.* Bel crossed her arms, leaned back against the car, and stared at him, her expression a mixture of amusement and frustration. She looked good, looked more than good, with her hair rumpled from his rough hands, her cheeks rosy, a hint of stubble burn at her throat. Her resilience floored him. She'd seen his family at their twisted worst and took everything in stride.

"You're fucking amazing, *ma belle*," he said, putting all his admiration for her in his voice.

"Damn straight I am. Now give me the keys and get furry."

His wolf grumbled at the indignity of squeezing into the confined space of the passenger side. Bel lowered the seat as far as it would go, and he managed to sprawl across it and half into the narrow rear seat of the convertible. He kept his head down, and Bel stuck to a few miles under the speed limit. Still, his hackles didn't soften until he felt the car bump onto the rougher roads, signaling they were back in Moonlight. Derek waited for them. Troy caught his scent the moment the car rolled to a stop a few feet from Bel's front door. The alpha strode from the shadows, raised one eyebrow at Troy in his wolf form, and tugged Bel into a tight hug. A wash of possessive jealousy rolled over Troy and he snarled, too worn down by the privations of the day to school his temper.

Derek released Bel, grabbed Troy by the scruff of his neck, and shook him hard. "Don't fucking test me, pup. When your car stopped so close to your father's lands, I feared there had been an ambush." The alpha softened his grip, stroking his hand over the wolf's head in a gesture of affection no other male had given him for twenty years. Not since the night Clark had changed everything. He turned in to the alpha's touch, seeking reassurance. Derek dropped to his haunches and caught Troy's muzzle in his hand. Golden eyes blazing, he stared deep at Troy. "You're mine now. He doesn't get to hurt you again; do you hear me?"

The vow rocked Troy to his core, giving him a flash of brief hope before reality dug its cruel claws into his heart. His father would hurt him again, and he would take the pain gladly to protect this noble wolf and his pack.

Chapter Ten

The next week flew past in a tumble of love, laughter, and lies. When Troy wasn't closeted with Derek and the rest of The Defenders running over every conceivable scenario of what might happen at the mating ceremony, he was on her, over her, in her. His appetite for her burned like a living flame, and desperation tinged their every encounter.

He stared into her eyes, pumping his seed into her body, telling her he loved her, making plans for their future together. And lied and lied until she thought she might choke on it. Something had changed during the hour he'd spent in his father's study. He'd given up on her, given up on them, she could tell.

She checked her watch. Troy and the others were prowling around the open ground behind the cottage. The grass had been mown, and a beautiful wooden pagoda dominated the center of the strip of land. Garlands of flowers and fairy lights twined around the open frame. It would be a magical setting for their mating ceremony and provide a precise location for the ambush of their guests from Brighton.

Watching from the rear porch, she saw Kirk leap up, grasp the lower branches of a tree on the edge of the wood, and vanish into the thick foliage. Jesse and Charlie, the human sheriffs who had mated into their pack, stared up into the branches, a large rifle strapped across Charlie's back. She turned away with a shudder. What should be the happiest night of her life lay a few hours ahead, and everywhere she looked her pack prepared for war.

She shook away the tears pricking the back of her eyes and stepped inside. Picking up her phone, she scrolled her contacts for Quinn's number. They'd talked often over the week, discussing plans for the ceremony, forging a connection they both needed. The line rang a couple of times, and Quinn answered it, sounding slightly breathless. "Hello?"

"Hi. Sorry, are you busy?" Bel sank onto the edge of the couch, nibbling on the corner of one fingernail. She caught her nervous action, tucking her newly manicured hand under her thigh to prevent any further abuse of the pearly pink lacquer Riesa had applied the night before. The alpha's mate and her other close female friends had thrown her a surprise party. Nothing extravagant, just a few drinks, home mani-pedis, and some ridiculous feel-good chick flicks. It should have been a special memory, something to cherish for years, and yet a pall of fear had hung over the group. How many of them would still have their mates happy and whole when this latest nightmare to challenge their pack was over?

She heard a whisper of material, a closing door, and Quinn sighed into the phone. "Just trying to get everything organized at this end. I'm having a wardrobe crisis. I swear I've tried on everything in my wardrobe. Twice." Her laugh settled some of Bel's nerves. "So what's up, sis? Cold feet?"

The affectionate acknowledgment of their new familial connection settled over Bel like a warm hug. Falling in love with Troy had brought her something she had never expected, had never realized she'd missed until she'd found it. Having a sister to share things with would be wonderful. If everything worked out okay.

"Has Troy spoken to you?" She tried to keep the gnawing fear out of her voice, knew she'd failed when she heard Quinn's intake of breath.

"What's he said to you?" There was something in the way she asked, some hesitation, and Bel knew her suspicions were correct.

"You know what he's planning, don't you?" There was more accusation than she'd meant in her words, but she couldn't help it. Troy was supposed to be her mate. They shouldn't be keeping secrets from one another.

A muffled thump echoed down the phone. "Shit, hold on," Quinn muttered. She turned away from the phone. "I'll be there in a minute, Nik. Hold your goddamn horses." Another sigh. "Look, Bel. I have to go. We'll be with you in a few hours. I can't tell you anything, but please know Troy is doing everything he can to keep you and your pack safe."

Cold fear squeezed her heart. "And what about his safety? What about your safety?"

A brittle laugh sent icy fingers down her spine. "Bel, darling. When you grow up Brighton, you learn something at a very young age. Safety is a pretty illusion. Nothing more."

The phone went dead in Bel's hand. She was still staring at the handset when a soft knock at the kitchen door stirred her.

Glancing up, she couldn't help but smile at her mate leaning against the frame. "You don't have to knock, Troy. This is your home now." He'd moved out of the guest cottage next door, freeing it up for his family to use during their visit.

He shrugged one shoulder, the dimple in his chin deepening when he gave her a sheepish smile. "I wasn't sure what you were up to. Didn't want to disturb you if you needed some quiet time before the ceremony."

Brackets of strain framed his bright-green eyes, a vein throbbed at his temple, and yet he looked at her like he could eat her up. She drew a deep breath into her lungs, took his essence deep within and made up her mind. If Troy thought she would let him make some kind of noble sacrifice in the hopes of saving her, then he would be sorely disappointed. They were mates, and she would fight for him. Fight for them with everything she had.

"Come here." She crooked her finger at him, inhaled again, and let the scent of eucalyptus, sweat, and all the other things that made him unique settle over her. He wore a pair of cut-off jean shorts and nothing else. Dirt and sweat streaked his torso, matting the trail of dark-brown hair on his lower belly into little curls. Stubble darkened his jaw, and his hair twisted every which way from where he'd scrubbed his hands through it and mopped the sweat from his brow. Primal, earthy, so unlike the urbane image he projected. This was the real Troy, and she loved him so much. The weight of her love for him, her fear for them both, filled her until her skin felt too tight. Her wolf rose, surging forward, responding to the woman's need. Hungry, so hungry for him. She needed to make him this hungry, too.

Licking her lower lip, she stripped her T-shirt over her head, the motion so fast it made her breasts bounce. Eyes locked on her chest, he prowled across the room, tipped her over his arm, and sucked her left breast into his mouth. *Yes. Good.* She raked her nails down his back, leaving a mark of wanton heat, giving him a sensation to replace any lingering memory of his father's beating. *Feel me, taste me, think only of me.* She shoved her hands into his shorts, gripped his firm ass, and pulled him into her body, grinding her sex against the solid heat of his erection. He growled, gave her the edge of his teeth, and she moaned his name. Working her hands around to the front, she pressed her palms against the lower ridges of his abdomen, teasing her fingers through the dark curls framing his cock. His body jerked in response, and he shifted his mouth from her breast to her collarbone, then on up to her throat to settle on the place she wore his mark.

Arching her neck, she offered herself, shivered when his teeth pressed deep, not quite breaking the skin. He shifted his hands, cupped her breasts, and pinched her nipples hard enough to distract her from her efforts to unfasten the fly of his shorts. Molten heat filled her core, and the spicy scent of her arousal filled the air, turning her on even more. Hard hands gripped her waist, and he lifted her onto the kitchen counter, stripping her bare in one hard rip of cotton. She would need to go underwear shopping soon if he kept destroying her panties. She scooted until she could feel the cool plaster of the wall at her back, lifted her feet onto the counter, heels braced on the edge. Tugging up the long, loose skirt she wore, she let the material pool at her hips, leaving her naked sex on full display to him. He licked his lips, eyes intent on the seam of her pussy. Using the fingers of one hand, she spread her lower lips, revealing the glistening entrance of her core, the tight pink bud of her clit.

"Give me your hand," she murmured, and his eyes flicked away from her sex with a hot questioning look. The eager glow she saw there proved she was on the right track. She'd let him take the lead, happy to give him her body whenever he reached for her, but she'd been passive, too acquiescent. He needed to know she craved him, too, craved this as much as he did.

Not waiting for him to respond, she grasped his hand, tugging it to her mouth. She licked the tip of his index finger then drew it between her lips. Sucking hard, she worked the length of his finger with her tongue, watched his cock twitch and jump in response. The heady sensation of witnessing his arousal spurred her on, and she stretched her mouth wider to take his middle finger in too, sliding up and down the digits, mimicking the hard pressure he loved when she sucked him off.

"Fuck, Bel," he groaned. "That's so hot, baby. You're killing me." He fisted the base of his cock, squeezed tight, but made no move toward her.

Pleased he continued to let her take the lead, she freed his fingers from her mouth, guided them down the center of her body, and pressed them into her core. Her head knocked back against the wall, but she didn't notice the pain, too caught up in the sensation of his wide fingers stretching her open. She pulled him back, pressed forward again, fucking herself with his hand. Eyes glued to him, she watched him watch her. A muscle twitched in his jaw, and a frown of concentration furrowed his brow as he stared between her legs.

The pressure built within her, but she needed more. A quick tug freed his fingers from her core, and she pressed them against her clit instead, circling the throbbing nub. She tangled their hands together, using a firmer, touch, rocking in time with the swift strokes. Her pussy clenched, the muscles empty and needy, but the pulsing demand in her clit would not be denied.

"Troy," she moaned his name, a sighing sob he had no trouble interpreting.

Dropping to his knees, he twisted his head to one side, ducking beneath their squirming hands to shove his tongue deep into her core. His free hand grabbed her leg, lifting it over his shoulder, giving himself enough room to press deeper until his lips formed a seal around the opening of her pussy. He worked her with his tongue, scissored his fingers on either side of her clit, and pinched hard, rocketing her lower body off the counter into his face.

A keening wail rose in her throat, building higher, louder with every thrust of his tongue. The hand on her leg slid lower, cupped her ass, and lifted her into his mouth, holding her tight so he could control her movements. The tip of his thumb brushed against the tight pucker of her anus, and it was one sensation too many. She tried to squirm away, and he growled fiercely, sending a rippling vibration through her whole core. Lights danced behind her closed eyelids, and she sobbed his name, the word choking off in a scream when he pressed the tip of his thumb into her ass, sending a spear of dark pleasure through her. Her orgasm battered through her like a storm, ripping her open, sending shards of awareness scattering so far she wasn't sure she could piece herself together again.

She felt him lift her, and the kiss of cold tile against her skin drew her back to awareness. The hot weight of his body caged her in, and he thrust hard, driving balls deep in that first desperate roll of his hips. The breath flew from her lungs, another ragged cry that filled the room with the sound of his name.

"Bel. Bel, fuck, Bel." He grunted her name at the apex of every thrust, punctuating the slap of his hips against her ass.

Bracing her head on her folded arms, she lifted up to meet him, too wired to come again, or so she thought. The hot flood of his seed bathing her core triggered another wave of pleasure, and she would have collapsed beneath it had the strong arms banded around her waist not held her up. Troy sank back on his thighs, tugging her with him until she splayed across his lap.

Her head lolled back on his shoulder, too heavy for her to hold up. He slid a hand up her body, encircled her throat in his wide grip, and supported her as they panted heavily against each other. Tears clogged her nose, burned behind her lids until she couldn't hold them back. A rasping sob burst from her.

"Don't leave me." She choked on the tears, let him turn her head until her face rested against cheek.

She hadn't meant to do this, hadn't meant to flay her soul open and show him how scared she was. Her oh-so-clever plan to show him what he had to live for had backfired spectacularly, revealing instead everything she stood to lose.

His cock softened, slipped from her body, and he twisted her around in his lap, catching her face between his hands. She couldn't look at him, couldn't bear to see his eyes, see the love he would soon deny her. His thumbs dug into her jaw, forcing her gaze to him. "Bel, *ma belle*. What is this?" he crooned, kissing the tears away from her cheeks.

"I'm going to lose you. You've shown me what it is to truly live, and now you're going to give up on us." She pulled free of his hold, scrubbing at her eyes until the hard press of her fingers stemmed the flow of tears.

"Bel." His groan of agony turned her sorrow to frustration again. She balled her fist, thumping him in the chest. The blow did nothing except make her fingers sting, so she struck him again. He grasped her hand, pressed it against his heart. "Please, baby."

"Tell me," she growled, and this time he was the one to turn his face away. "Tell me, Troy."

He shook his head, and something inside her snapped. Burrowing deep within him, she sifted the threads of his emotions, touching and tasting each one, tracing them to the very depths of his soul. He struggled to push her away, mentally and physically, but she clung on, wrapping the fingers of her free hand around the back of his neck, her legs around his waist, locking their bodies together. Pulling at the threads of her own soul, she sorted the strands, matching their emotions, weaving them together into a gossamer net. For every negative in one, she found the positive in the other. His clawing fear of his father, her faith in him to find a way to survive, her quiet doubt she could be a strong enough mate for him, his burning love for her. She stripped them bare, gave him all her weaknesses, took his without flinching, showing them both they could be so much more together. His struggles subsided, and his arms wrapped tight around her, clutching her hard enough to strain her ribs. A shudder rippled through him. Another.

He lifted his head. "I'm going to challenge him," he whispered, and her heart thudded. Her mate, her true heart was no alpha. They both knew it. A beta to his core, his role should be to nurture and protect his pack mates. She was no alpha's mate either. But she would be, if she had to. She couldn't join the fight. An alpha challenge was single combat, winner take all. Those were the rules.

Fuck the rules.

His eyes widened in response to the fierce whisper she sent into his mind. He nodded once, and a clarity of purpose spread out through the web binding them together. They were one. They would survive or fall together.

Her blood was up, and her wolf had its prey fixed firmly in its sights. Clark would not be allowed to win. "How do we do this?"

Chapter Eleven

Troy couldn't help but smile as Bel wove her way through the gathered members of her pack toward him. Each one held a single flower, which they handed to her in turn, together with a hug, a kiss, a smile, or a word of blessing. Her bare feet showed beneath the flowing hem of the simple lilac-colored gown she wore, and a garland of flowers held her hair back from her forehead. Crystals studded the dress, catching the light as she twisted and turned through the circle her pack mates had formed around the central pagoda. His darling girl loved to sparkle.

His family stood to the left of him. Troy glanced across, spotting the possessive look on Clark's face as he, too, watched Bel make her way toward them. *Look your fill, old man. I'll never let you near her.* The angry thought melted away as his mate brushed her mind against his. He would need every ounce of his fury soon enough, no point in wasting it now.

Dutton and Nikolas bracketed their father, both dressed in loose pants and collarless tunics, the same as Troy. Bel had wanted a casual feel, a relaxed atmosphere rather than anything too formal. The loose-fitting clothing worn by the pack would make it easier to fight, easy to shred the light material if they needed to shift. His father had insisted on a jacket and tie. Putting appearance over comfort summed up everything Clark stood for. He would be made to regret it soon enough.

She mounted the three low stairs to the dais and handed the huge bouquet of flowers to Riesa, who brushed a kiss to Bel's cheek and surreptitiously left the raised area to stand between Alexa and Liana. The two wolves, mates to the human sheriffs who hid in the trees, would protect their alpha's mate at all costs. The rest of the humans were not present, their lives too precious and too easily taken to risk them in the field of combat. His father had been unable to hide his disdain for Derek when he'd discovered the other alpha had mated a human. An unforgivable weakness in his eyes.

Derek stepped forward, cupped Bel's cheek, and drew her close enough to press a kiss to her forehead. Troy watched his mate close her eyes, felt her draw strength and courage from her alpha through the magical web she'd woven between them. It was a mate bond unlike anything he'd ever heard about. Flexible, yet strong, it gave him all the reassurance he needed. They had not yet taken the final step in a full mating—had not come together in their wolf forms— but they were a unit. He could sense her wolf, feel the way it calmed and soothed the beast within him, holding it in check. The Moonlight alpha took Bel's hand, led her to where Troy waited, and clasped his hand in turn. He stood between the two of them, connecting them, showing he accepted Bel's choice of mate.

You need to shift to the right; you're blocking Charlie's line of sight. The smile of benediction on Derek's face never wavered as he gave the instruction to Troy. The plan the pack had put together would see Derek take on Clark. Rand would target Dutton, and Kirk stood at the base of the steps, ready to pounce on Nikolas. Jesse and Charlie would shoot only if necessary. No one wanted to put the humans in a position where they would have to commit a crime, but they had been insistent. When it came to dealing with wolves, the normal rules didn't apply—pack was all. They'd butted their way into the defense plans and would not be moved.

Raising their linked arms, Derek brought them together, pressing Bel and Troy palm to palm, clasping their now joined hands within his own. "Fates blessing on you both. May you always run free, hunt well, love fierce, stay true." Simple words, said with great feeling, and Troy bowed his head to acknowledge them. The alpha released them, stepped back, and adopted an outwardly casual stance next to Rand, his second.

Tears glistened at the corner of Bel's eyes, and her fingers squeezed his. They were so small and delicate compared to his, but her grip was sure. He focused on his love for her. The net between them pulsed in response, and she met his gaze. The bright-blue look she fixed on him floored him. What had he done to deserve her? He could spend every day of the next century showing her how grateful he was for her and it would never be enough.

"I love you." He blurted the words, sending a ripple of laughter around the ring of watching wolves.

She flung herself into his arms, almost knocking him over with the force of her jump. He captured her lips, and they parted for him, welcoming the thrust of his tongue. Sliding his hands lower, he cupped the round cheeks of her ass, drawing her against the aching heat of the front of his body. Instantly aflame for her, he forgot everything but his desire, the eager leap of her own as it rose to meet his, stoking and feeding the fire.

"Get a room, you two." Rand's drawled remark and the chuckles it drew from the others broke through the haze.

Troy lifted his head reluctantly. Bel blinked up at him, pink lips soft and glistening wet, and he dipped his head to claim her again. Their mouths hovered inches apart when another voice intruded, dashing his lust in a bucket of cold fear.

"Don't you wish to seek my blessing, too, son?" Clark's mock-scolding tone was an attempt at levity, but Troy could hear the anger in it. They'd ignored him for too long. Allowing Derek to conduct the joining of their hands had been his right. They stood upon his pack lands, but Clark wouldn't see it that way. In his mind, he already owned the wolves around him.

Releasing his hold on Bel, he kept her hand planted firmly in his as they turned to face the Brighton alpha. Troy cast a glance toward Quinn, read the pain and pride on her face, and swallowed hard. She would be the first to suffer at Clark's hand if things went south.

Clark beamed at them both, black eyes bright with madness. The acrid stink of his twisted scent rose, a sure sign he stood on the cusp of his control.

Holding out his hand to Bel, Clark spoke, raising his voice to carry far beyond the dais. "Let me welcome you, daughter. The newest member of my pack and soon to be my greatest asset."

"That's not what we agreed." Derek growled, and the wooden planks beneath Troy's feet vibrated as he felt the Moonlight alpha move closer behind him.

"Did you really think I would suffer another pack so close to my territory?" Clark sneered, ignoring Troy to glare past him at Derek. "There is only one alpha in the Southern states, and you are looking at him." Clark clicked his fingers at Dutton, who lifted the cell phone he held unobtrusively at his side.

"Now." Dutton didn't look at Clark, didn't look at anyone other than Troy as he issued the command. He might have spoken into the handset, but the single word was aimed at Troy. *Quinn told us,* Dutton's voice whispered in his head.

Releasing Bel's hand, Troy shoved her hard behind him into the safety of Derek's arms. Wolves poured from every direction, filling the air with snarls and howls, forming a ring of death around the gathered members of the Moonlight pack. Clark raised his arm, eyes glowing hot, ready to give the signal to attack.

"Challenge," Troy said, his calm voice at odds with the racing of his heart. It would have been nice to savor the look of utter shock on his father's face for a few moments, but there was no time. Throwing his head back, he summoned the power of his wolf and roared again. "Challenge!"

The shouts and snarls of men and wolves fell silent, and everyone turned to him.

"What is this nonsense?" Clark snapped. "Don't

be ridiculous, boy. You are not fit to lick my boots, never mind challenge me."

"It is my right to seek challenge; you must answer or forfeit. What do you say?" He didn't dare look away, could hear Bel whispering behind him, explaining the change of plan to Derek, but he couldn't risk turning to seek her out. He caught a movement from the corner of his eye, the solid form of Nikolas easing away from Quinn's side.

A vicious grin twisted Clark's face into a mask of ugly hate. "Fine. I'll kill you, claim your mate as my own, and force this excuse of an alpha to stand by while I slaughter any wolf of his who refuses to bow their head to me."

Troy took a step back, not in retreat, but to shift the two of them to the center of the dais. He heard a growl to his left, knew Derek would be furious at him for blocking Charlie's line of sight again. This was his fight, and he would not allow the human sheriff to interfere. He paused, giving his father a chance to slip off his shoes, shrug off his jacket, and toss it casually toward Dutton. The alpha's attention was too closely fixed on Troy to notice that Dutton let the coat drop to the floor at his feet, but Troy spotted it. The act of disrespect gave him hope. Maybe his brothers wouldn't stand against him in this. Maybe they understood they, too, had the faintest chance of escaping Clark's evil clutches. But only if Troy could defeat him.

He tested his weight on the balls of his feet, shook the tension from his hands, and lowered to a crouch. The gentle influence of Bel's wolf slipped away in his mind, letting his own animal rise to the fore, filling his blood and body with long-suppressed aggression. Too often had they submitted to this monster. Too often had they bled and hurt to protect the weaker members of the pack. They would bleed again today, but nothing would stay their hand.

Clark paced back and forth before him, feinting left then right, trying to draw Troy to attack, but he held his ground. Sweat popped on the alpha's brow, and a low rumbling growl rolled in his throat. He shook his head in irritation, and Troy schooled himself not to react. He'd disagreed when she first suggested it, but Bel had been adamant she would play her part. She would turn her ability on Clark, drive his aggression higher, try to send him off balance and force him to lose his temper.

The alpha snarled, bared his teeth at Troy, and pounced, swinging his huge fist in a clubbing blow, which caught his shoulder, knocking him to one knee. *Shit*. His arm hung numb at his side, the force of the punch stunning his nerves. He rose quickly, ducked a second attack, and rammed his elbow into Clark's gut, driving a gust of air from his lungs. Panting and snarling, the alpha charged him, taking Troy to the floor in a rain of claws and teeth. There was no time for finesse, for planning his next move, there was only the need to strike and strike again, try to draw as much blood as possible before the gouges in his own flesh weakened him.

Troy battled on, knowing the calmness in his mind was thanks to his mate. She took his pain, damping it down and stoking his courage, holding him in the web of her love. Taking the strength she gave him, he heaved Clark away from him, pushed to his feet, stumbled and fell when his leg collapsed beneath him. A gaping hole at his ankle gushed blood, his foot hung at an awkward angle. *Fuck*. Clark had hobbled him.

Staring through the sweaty strands of hair on his forehead, Troy watched the alpha circle him. He forced himself to follow, scrambling on his knees to avoid letting Clark get behind him. Adrenaline faded, and his mind catalogued his injuries. He tried to ignore the pain, using his arms and his one good leg to keep in motion, to not be an easy target. A flash of lilac caught his eye, and he spotted Bel over Clark's shoulder. Derek held her straining body back as she struggled to escape. Their eyes met.

I'm sorry, ma belle.

Don't give up, Troy. Don't you ever give up.

A flood of strength washed over him, driving the pain to the far reaches of his mind. His relief was short-lived. He watched in horror as Bel swayed in Derek's arms. Her eyes rolled back, and she slumped to the floor. The web between them vanished, leaving him alone in his mind.

His scream split the air in a roar of loss, of rage and defeat. He had nothing left to live for. Calling to his wolf, Troy gathered every ounce of strength his mate had given him and threw himself at Clark. Hard hands grabbed him, stopping his exhausted body in mid-leap. Bands of steel crushed the air from his lungs, and he snarled as the familiar scent of Nikolas filled his nose. The alpha's hammer held him tight, Troy's spitting accusations of betrayal and rage sliding off him. Dutton moved into his line of sight, and Troy broke. He'd given them the chance and they hadn't taken it. Had stayed loyal to a man who didn't deserve it, who had given them nothing but pain in return for their loyalty.

Clark swiped the sweat from his face, turned his head, and spat a gob of blood and mucus at Bel's body where she lay on the dais at Derek's feet. The filthy mess spattered over the beautiful fabric of her gown, and Troy had to close his eyes, unable to bear the sight of his fallen mate.

"Kill them, kill them all!" Clark snarled, and his pack howled in response, driven by his bloodlust.

"Hold!" Dutton raised his clenched fist, and the baying Brighton wolves fell silent. Troy forced his head up, watching in disbelief as his brother placed himself between Troy and Clark. What was this now? "Clark Lansing," Dutton's voice rang cold and clear. "I repudiate you. No father to me, no alpha to me. You are nothing."

Clark staggered as though from a blow, and Dutton bent at the waist, gasping for air.

"Clark Lansing," Nikolas's deep voice rumbled deep against Troy's back. "I repudiate you." His growling tone was matched with another softer one as Quinn stepped up beside them. She placed her hand on Nik's arm where it banded across Troy's chest, holding him up. Their voices rose in unison. "No father to me, no alpha to me. You are nothing." Nik grunted in pain, but he somehow managed to keep hold of Troy and grab Quinn when she collapsed.

"No!" Clark's voice twisted in a painful scream.

Pushing free of his brother's hold, Troy hopped forward, rested his hand on Dutton's back as his brother emptied his stomach on the floor. "Clark Lansing," he rasped. "I repudiate you. No father to me, no alpha to me. You are nothing."

The alpha bond severed, sending him crashing to

the floor. Bright pain sparked through his nerve endings, and the edges of his vision blurred. His pulse throbbed in his ears, and he focused on each dull beat, counting the growing spaces between each one. He closed his eyes, listening to his father's screams of pain and fear, and smiled.

Over the fading sounds of his heart, the sobbing pleas of his father, the voices of his pack rose as one damning chorus. "Clark Lansing. We repudiate you...."

He'd done enough. He couldn't save himself, couldn't save his Bel, but they'd both agreed death would be a price worth paying to save their packs. His wolf keened in his mind, and he tried to soothe it. They would claim their mate soon enough. Would spend eternity running free together in the lands beyond.

Epilogue

Soft lips brushed his cheek, and Troy turned onto his side. A cool breeze blew through the open windows, stirring the drapes, making them flutter in the pale rays of the full moon. He stroked his hand down the length of Bel's spine, delighting in the shudder of pleasure rippling in the wake of his touch.

The top her plump ass peeked from beneath the white cotton sheet draping her lower half. He nudged it free and leaned forward to place a teasing kiss to one cheek, making her giggle. Using his teeth, he pressed into the ripe flesh, turning her giggle to a gasp then a moan as he dipped his fingers between her legs and tested her readiness. Wet for him. It never ceased to amaze him how her body primed itself so readily for his touch. He trailed lower, delved into the heat of her core, felt her arch beneath the press of his mouth against her ass.

A howl echoed through the open window, followed by another and another until the voices of the Brighton pack thrummed in his veins, calling to him. His pack was ready to run. Their first run together under the control of their new alpha.

Dutton had brought sweeping changes to Brighton in the weeks Troy had lain recuperating, first in Bel's house at Moonlight and then here at home. Derek had agreed to release Bel temporarily once she'd recovered from the flame out that nearly killed her. Only her alpha's stubborn refusal to relinquish her had kept her alive. He'd called the pack to him, drawn on their collective strength to hold her to them.

Dutton had formally requested their assistance. He had been working behind the scenes for months, using his network of spies to make allies among the subservient packs, seeking out potential alphas who could assume control if he found a way to break them free of Clark's hold. Once Quinn had gone to him and Nikolas, told them of Troy's planned challenge and begged them for help, Dutton had seized the opportunity and put his plan into action. Every wolf who had once bowed their head to Clark had broken from him, suffered agony to do so, but none had waivered. The sudden loss of power had destroyed what was left of Clark's mind, and Dutton had finished him with a sharp twist of his neck, showing more mercy than his father ever had.

The broken packs were holding—just. Troy and Bel were needed to bolster the most fragile of them. They'd use his beta diplomacy and her omega skills to settle the ruffled fur and help the new alphas find their way. Nikolas and Quinn were already out there, showing solidarity, forming friendships where once only ties of fear had held the packs of Brighton together. No one would be forced to remain within the group, but it was hoped most would. Dutton howled again, and the pack beneath their window raced away, their cries and yips echoing in the night.

Bel wriggled her ass, pressed herself hard onto his hand then twisted away. He growled, rising onto his knees to stalk her across the wide expanse of their bed. His damaged ankle had healed but would never be right. Troy limped in both human and wolf forms, but his mate didn't seem to care.

She raised her hands over her head, stretching her lithe body in the moonlight. His mouth watered at the sight of her. "It's time," she murmured."

He nodded. Their wolves had waited long enough. It was time to complete the last step in their mating. Taking her hand, he led his mate through the house, down the wide sweeping stairs, and out the front door. He wanted to show her the land, show her his favorite places. The shallow creek with the thick mossy banks. The best places to hunt rabbits. Dropping to his knees, he summoned his wolf, letting the power of the full moon ease his shift from man to beast.

They ran for hours, teasing and pouncing on each other until the need between them built to unbearable levels. He chased her south, driving her toward the creek. Sides heaving, they flopped onto the cushion of moss, lapping at the cool water of the creek. Turning toward her, Troy pressed his muzzle deep into the thick fur at her throat, drawing the luscious scent of his mate deep into his lungs. Her arousal bloomed strong and steady in the heavy night air, and he watched as Bel rose to her paws and turned, offering her rear to him. He licked her, tasting the darker musk of her wolf body, driving them both crazy with need. Rising on his hind legs, he mounted her carefully, easing his aching cock into the hot depths of her sex. She adjusted her body under his weight, bracing herself better to take the urgent thrusts of his hips. A low growl rose in his throat, and he clamped his jaws into the thick ruff of her neck, holding her in place. The web connection pulsed brighter, and her pussy spasmed around him, drawing his seed from his body, the final piece of their mating connection slotting in place.

Throwing back his head, Troy howled his pleasure to the skies. His mate raised her voice with him, and they sang of their love, their union, their hunger for each other to the watching moon.

About the Author

Merryn Dexter is a military spouse who, after a varied employment career (from selling sandals to old ladies with bunions to being a health and safety coordinator for a construction company), is thrilled to be pursuing her dream career as a romance writer. She likes The Winchesters, Spike, Hotch, Loki and watching complicated European Noir. Her hobbies include crying at books, crying at movies, crying at tv serials (there's a theme!) and believes all stories should have a Happy Ending.

Also by Merryn Dexter

A Mate's Healing Touch
A Mate's Redeeming Touch
Soul of Flame
Mating Dance
Silver Moon